THE DREAM KEEPER

A. B. COHEN

First paperback edition December 2018

ISBN 9781791719685

For Prof. Garber, who saw me first.
For Nissim, Mari, and Nats, my first readers.
For Marcos Z"L, my best friend.

CHAPTER 1

THE FORD PROBE was eating the road at 90 mph. It was already past 7:30 a.m. Daniel Spence took the exit towards Ashfield, Massachusetts. He drove through the small town, passing a grocery store, a high school, a small nursery and, of course, a church.

My God, how could someone live here? wondered Daniel as he took a right and saw a small creek bordering the town. He speculated on how mundane life would be in a place like this: working on the land or in a coal mine during the week, high school football on Friday night, the farmers' market every other week, and church on Sunday.

Now the road was flanked by trees—pine trees decorated with snow. Daniel took a left, leaving the creek behind him, and went on a stretch of road through the forest. Before long, he reached the entrance of a fenced area. He could see what seemed to be a two-level concrete structure ahead.

A guard—a blond, white man in his forties who rocked a mustache—came out of the security cabin and approached him.

"Good morning. My name is Daniel Spence. I'm assuming this is the entrance to The Cooper Institute. I have an interview scheduled for this morning."

The guard looked at him with disdain. "ID and pass code please."

"Oh yeah, sure." He reached for his folder on the passenger seat and took out a page with his temporary access code. "Here you go."

The guard took Daniel's documentation and went inside. After a couple of minutes, he came out, took his license plate number, gave him back his documents, and let him through. Daniel parked his car in the parking lot and pulled down the sun visor to check himself in the mirror. His green eyes looked back at him as he groomed his black hair with his fingers. Daniel stepped out and felt the cold air reach his lungs. He straightened his shirt, put on his blazer, grabbed his folder, and walked through the revolving doors with confidence.

The smell of coffee dominated the warm air of the lobby. Rays of early-morning sun penetrated the glass wall and illuminated a very simple space. A high ceiling, a leather couch on each side of the room, a small clock on the wall, and the front desk. Behind it sat a woman with short, black hair reading from a Macintosh Classic II, biting the end of her pencil.

"Good morning. I'm Daniel Spence. I'm here for an interview with Dr. Cooper at eight thirty."

The secretary looked up. Her striking hazel eyes penetrated Daniel.

"Good morning, Mr. Spence. Welcome to The Cooper Institute. Yes, we were expecting you. Please have a seat. The doctor will be with you in just a moment. Would you like some coffee? The new pot should be done soon."

"Coffee sounds wonderful, thanks," Daniel responded with a smile.

He sat in one of the couches and went over his notes. His leg shook a little with impatience, and he started to sweat as last-minute nerves kicked in. This opportunity could be a big jump in his professional and academic career and could potentially allow him to bury some of the mistakes that had clouded his résumé the past couple of years.

"Mr. Spence, coffee is ready."

Daniel snapped out of his thoughts and approached the desk. The young woman was concentrating on her computer, still biting the end of the pencil. Daniel grabbed the cup from the counter.

I guess black is fine.

"Thank you very much, Mrs....?"

She barely turned toward him. "Mrs. Kelly Marshall." She gave him a quick forced smile and returned to the computer.

He went back to his seat, sipping from the hot cup. Daniel reread some of his responses to basic questions in his notes. Questions like "Why are you the best option for the job?" and "What are you looking to gain out of this opportunity?" were underlined in red and followed by an opening line and a set of bullet points. Every now and then, a specific sentence was highlighted, and he rehearsed it in his head. Truth was that Daniel has been preparing for this interview since he received news of it a couple of months ago. For him, this was a golden opportunity to finally work for someone other than his father and leave the past in the past.

Not more than five minutes later, Kelly called for him. "Dr. Cooper is ready for you, Mr. Spence. Please follow me."

"Great, thanks." Daniel followed her through a thick frosted-glass door. The hallway was small and a bit tight. Its white walls, low acoustic ceilings, and white fluorescent lights gave the impression of a very sterile place. They created a funnel effect from the lobby that made him uncomfortable, claustrophobic.

As he followed Kelly, Daniel instinctively checked her out. Her long, thin legs and well-defined butt were simply perfect. He forced himself to look up.

Come on, Spence, focus. You'll have time for that later.

They stopped in front of a wooden door to their left, and Kelly knocked.

"Come in, come in," said a relaxed voice from inside.

"Mr. Spence, so good to finally meet you." An old man, probably in his sixties, stood up from behind a beautiful dark wooden desk. He wore a lab coat and greeted Daniel with a smile.

"It's an honor to meet you, Dr. Cooper."

They shook hands firmly as he looked into the old man's blue eyes.

"Not every day you get to meet the man behind the legend," Daniel said, following that with his best PR smile.

They both sat down, and even though Daniel tried to be focused, he could not help but notice the creepy large painting hanging behind the desk of a woman dressed in white, sleeping on her back with her arms and head hanging off the bed. A creature sat on the woman's belly, and a black horse with white eyes peeked from behind a red curtain behind her. Daniel was sure he had seen it somewhere but could not remember the name.

"First of all, welcome to The Cooper Institute," said Dr. Cooper. "How was the drive here this morning? You came from Boston. Correct?"

"Yes, it was pretty nice, actually. Love the beautiful small town," Daniel responded, taking a quick glimpse at the desk in an attempt to ignore the eerie painting. That was when he noticed a small picture of a girl, no more than six years old, with strong blue eyes and curly blond hair. Her sweet smile made Daniel smile slightly and helped him regain his focus.

"Ah yes, indeed. Ashfield might not seem like much at first, but it was an ideal location for The Cooper Institute." Dr. Cooper put his hands together and rested them on the desk. "So, why are you here, Mr. Spence?"

The highlighted question from his cheat sheet popped into his brain, along with the answer he had rehearsed. Daniel smiled with confidence.

"Because I believe I'm the most qualified person you will find. Being honored with the Olivia Sponsorship, and being able to work with you, one of the biggest influences in modern psychology, is an amazing opportunity. There is a lot of knowledge here at The Cooper Institute; your research and discoveries from the last two decades are way ahead of their time. But I also have a lot to offer: strong leadership skills, a methodical approach to problems, and a lot of experience in the field. I can go over specific examples if you like."

"Oh no, that won't be necessary," Dr. Cooper responded

with a gesture of his hand. "Tell me a bit more about yourself. What should I know about the son of the famous Dr. Robert Spence?" He smiled.

Classic annoying question.

"Since I was a little kid, I've been exposed to psychology by my father. I would hang out at his office and play around. So it was just a natural transition for me to follow in his footsteps. I went to Harvard for undergrad, and now I'm a PhD candidate. My research is focused on cognition, the brain, and behavior." Daniel tried to show some enthusiasm; it was not easy to live in the shadow of the famous Dr. Spence.

"Yes, yes, I saw that in your résumé, very impressive." Dr. Cooper leaned back in his chair and continued with his calm but firm voice. "Now, let's make a deal, Mr. Spence. Let's not lie to each other, shall we? I'll start. No kid in his right mind would fall in love with psychology through the teachings of someone like your father, especially in his later years."

Daniel clenched his fist below the table.

Dr. Cooper cleared his throat. "Forgive me if I'm blunt here, but I do not give a damn about your exaggerated stories, nor do I care about the rehearsed answers you've been practicing or even the diplomas your last name has given you. The same way that I don't care about your past mistakes and how you had some drug issues in your earlier years in college."

Daniel's face flushed with anger and surprise.

Dr. Cooper leaned forward with a serious expression on his face. "What I want to know, Mr. Spence, is if you are willing to seek the truth tirelessly after I tell you that everything you think you know about the human mind is a lie."

CHAPTER 2

THEY BOTH REMAINED silent and exchanged looks.

"Sorry to say this, Dr. Cooper, but for me to believe that, I would need proof and hard data. I'm not going to take your word for it just because of your role in the industry. You think that"—he paused to level his voice—"all my achievements come from my last name? You know me for five minutes and you already conclude that? And expect me to blindly believe a statement like that?"

Dr. Cooper grinned, and Daniel felt heat in his face and ears.

"Well, then, let's take a step back. I understand that this can be hard to believe. Why don't we start by talking about it? How do the mind and the brain relate to each other?"

Daniel crossed his arms and though for a moment, still irritated. "I would say that the mind enables us to be aware of the world around us and our experiences. If we follow the theory of monism—specifically, materialism, which is in my opinion the most dominant one—then we can say that the mind is just one more function of the brain. So the simple answer is they are one and the same."

"And what about the not-so-simple answer?" Dr. Cooper's wise, soft voice was both patient and assertive.

"I think that's more of a philosophical question. Believing the mind is separate from the brain would mean there is something beyond the physical world. Take this simple example: a subject is walking down the steps. He slips, falls, and hits his head. He passes out, meaning his brain goes off line, meaning his mind—his awareness—gets disconnected. So, I will put my money on logic and hard evidence."

"I see, but have you asked what is happening with his mind while he is unconscious?"

"Well, it just stops working."

"Really? How do you know that?"

"The person will say that the last thing he remembers is falling and then waking up."

"So, we are leaving that portion of the experiment to the subject's interpretation? We are basically assuming the subject has the right judgment in his situation. Why not instead develop a way to gather data and analyze what is happening inside his head while he is passed out? We can even go further and develop a process that will allow us to see what his mind sees while in that state."

"I would say that now you are adding a bit of science fiction to the story." Daniel leaned back in his seat, keeping his arms crossed.

"Am I? Or am I looking ahead? What was once science fiction later becomes science fact." He smiled and placed his arms on the desk, steepling his fingers. "You see, Mr. Spence, we have been taught that there are two ways of thinking: inside of the box and outside of the box. Well, at The Cooper Institute we have a very peculiar way of looking at things. We don't avoid the impossible, we embrace it. We don't take assumptions for granted, we question them—we question everything. Thinking outside of the box? More like wondering whether it's really a box."

Daniel remained silent at first, looking at the old man, trying to digest everything he just said. "Let's assume I see what you mean. How does that helps prove that everything I know about the mind is a lie?"

"It helps to recognize that the tools we have been using to test our theories are not efficient."

Daniel's eyes widened as he unfolded his arms and placed them on the desk. "So, then, you are saying that The Cooper Institute has invented a tool, or set of tools, that can more accurately study the human mind."

"Let me give you a hypothetical situation to illustrate my point. I believe it will help us finish this argument." He paused for a couple of seconds, as if to gather and organize his thoughts. "Imagine you are a part of a tribe in the jungle and you find a radio. You see a box with voices emerging from it. After a bit of experimentation, you realize that when you pull out some cables the voices become garbled. You have never dreamed of something called electromagnetic radiation. Eventually, you become an expert and develop theories on using the radio. Then you get stuck, because you say, 'Well, I can make all these correlations between the cables and the voices that it produces. But then when asked 'Why does this configuration of wires makes voices?,' you say, 'Well, that's the part I don't yet understand.' And you defend your position passionately because neither you nor the rest of your tribe can possibly imagine that there are large radio towers beaming radio signals everywhere.

So could it be that the brain is just the receptor of something else?"

Daniel remained silent. Dr. Cooper smiled, leaning back in his chair.

"My point is, Mr. Spence, that science is a complex collection of terms that allows us to explain the unexplainable. But like any other invention by humanity, it has its flaws. The main problem with it is that it does not allow us to look beyond it. It narrows our view and does not accept things that are outside the spectrum of measurement."

A silent exchange of looks took place. Finally, Daniel spoke in a more relaxed voice, opening his arms in a friendly gesture. "All right, Dr. Cooper, I think that is a very good argument, and I can see where you are going with this. I do have to say, though, I don't understand why you went from insulting everything I've achieved to this compelling discussion."

"Oliver Wendell Holmes Sr. was one of the best regarded American poets of the nineteenth century. He said, 'To obtain a man's opinion of you, make him mad.' I happen to believe in that. I did not want you to tell me what I wanted to hear; I wanted you to tell me what you really thought. It is hard to find that type of honesty during a first interview, so I pushed your buttons a bit." He smirked.

Daniel fidgeted uncomfortably in his seat.

The old man took out a silver pocket watch from his lab coat and glanced at it. "Our time is almost over. I'm happy to say that you will be joining us this summer. Now, do you have any questions for me before your departure?"

"Hold on a sec. I mean, this looks interesting and I can

see your vision, but I still don't know what I'll be doing here. What would my job consist of? What is expected of me?"

Dr. Cooper bent down and took a brown sealed folder from his drawer. "There isn't much I can tell you. Our experiments are top secret, and we are partially sponsored by the government, so my hands are tied. Now, a couple of things you need to know." He cleared his throat, then continued. "First, you will see there is a disclosure agreement on the last page. I'm required by law to tell you that anything we do at the institute has to stay within these walls. We do not want to bite the hand that feeds us. Second, we do a graveyard shift at The Cooper Institute, meaning we work at night and sleep during the day. You have one night break on Saturday, where you can leave the institute if you like. I expect all my researchers to be back by six thirty Sunday. You'll be staying at the institute. We have a cafeteria that runs 24/7." He handed over the folder. "This is your contract. Things are better explained there, but it mostly goes over the logistics of the sponsorship. You can sign it and bring it back on your first day. Just give us a call to confirm your acceptance in the next month." The old man stood up, and Daniel followed suit.

"All right, I think that's it for now," Dr. Cooper said.

They shook hands.

"Thank you for your time. I'll review the contract and get back to you as soon as possible."

Dr. Cooper's wrinkled lips curved up into a smile. "I believe we agreed on not lying to each other, Mr. Spence."

On his way back, Daniel could not stop thinking about what was probably the strangest and most intriguing interview he had ever had. He was not sure what to make of Dr. Cooper, who seemed to be either crazy or five steps ahead of everyone else. In his gut he believed it was a combination of both. Regardless, there was more to learn about the old man, and he knew who could give him more insight: his father. With one hand on the wheel, he grabbed his new Nokia 2140 Orange 5.0—the newest one on the market. He kept it in his hand for a bit, weighing his options. Finally, he took a deep breath and dialed.

"Dr. Spence's office. This is Lisa speaking. How can I help you?"

"Hi, Lisa, could you put my father on the line please?" Daniel said with a fake sweet voice.

"Just one second, Mr. Spence. He is finishing up with a patient. Would you like to wait or leave a message?"

"I'll wait, thanks."

Daniel was put on hold. He switched to the left lane and went faster. The radio was playing "The Show Must Go On" by Queen when a deep voice answered the phone.

"Dr. Spence speaking."

"Hey, Dad." He lowered the volume of the radio.

"Hey, Daniel. How did the interview go?"

"It went…well, I guess. Dr. Cooper is definitely a strange man."

"Did you receive an offer?"

"Yeah."

"Then that's all that matters. When are you starting?"

He assumes I'm accepting the offer just like that?

"Not sure yet. We haven't defined that. Probably sometime in mid-May…Dad, how long have you known Dr. Cooper?"

"I used to help him with research in the seventies. I must say I'm surprised he offered you this opportunity. I'm glad you'll get some work experience that is not in my office for a change."

"Yeah, it will be nice to learn from someone as influential as him for a change." Daniel wanted to remain silent and savor his comeback, but there were pressing questions, so he continued. "What do you think of him?"

"What do I think? I think you should not be judging the man who's giving you a job, Daniel."

"I'm not judging," Daniel said. "I just wanted to know what you think of him."

"He is a brilliant man, very smart, very charismatic. You'll learn a lot from this opportunity."

"All right, good to know." He pressed down on the gas, gaining speed rapidly. "Dad, you didn't ask him to give me a job, did you?"

A couple of seconds went by, and then his dad responded. "Not this time. For once you have achieved something on your own. Considering the mistakes you have made, I'm surprised you still get job offers. So don't screw this up, and don't bite the hand that feeds you."

I bet you can't reach the bottom.

Daniel pushed the thought away, took a deep breath, and tried to control his voice. "Thanks, Dad, I'll talk to you later."

His dad hung up without responding.

He is such an asshole.

Daniel turned up the music as Freddy Mercury was hitting a high note and put his foot on the gas.

I'll show the fucker what I'm made of.

CHAPTER 3

THE DOORS CLOSED behind Daniel, cutting off the warm air of summer, as he went into the lobby. He expected to see the attractive secretary again but was disappointed when he found an old lady, probably in her sixties, instead.

"Good afternoon. I'm Daniel Spence, the new intern."

The woman looked up and smiled kindly. "Mr. Spence, welcome. Dr. Cooper notified me of your arrival. Please follow me." She buzzed the door, and Daniel walked in, transitioning from the spacious lobby into the narrow hallway, and again a claustrophobic feeling tickled his spine, like he was entering a tunnel to another world. The old woman took a closer look at him, and then his bag. Her brown eyes seemed twice as big as they really were behind her thick, square glasses.

"Oh please, leave your bag next to my door, dear. The staff will take it to your room."

"All right, thank you."

They went down the hallway, passing Dr. Cooper's office, and took a left. The secretary knocked on a white door and peeked inside. "Sorry for the interruption, Dr. Cooper. Mr. Spence is here."

"Excellent. Let him in. Thank you, Nancy," Dr. Cooper said from inside.

She turned around, smiling, and opened the door for Daniel. He thanked her and walked in. Dr. Cooper stood in front of a blackboard with a bunch of annotations, like a professor giving a lecture. Daniel recognized Kelly, who was sitting next to two other guys around an oval table. They all wore lab coats and seemed to be taking notes.

"Welcome back, Mr. Spence. You are right on time." The old man approached him and they shook hands.

"Pleasure to see you again, Dr. Cooper."

Dr. Cooper smiled and turned toward the others. "Everyone, this is the newest addition to our team as I mentioned earlier, Mr. Daniel Spence."

The three of them stood up and greeted him as Dr. Cooper introduced Daniel to everyone around the table. He first met a man with strong features and dark hair, probably in his mid-forties. He had a scar that went from the left side of his forehead down to his chin that would've given him an intimidating look if it wasn't for his glasses, which gave him a more intellectual feel.

"This is Dr. Viktor Cowen. He has been with me for... what is it now? Nine years, Viktor?"

"Ten as of last month, Dr. Cooper," he said with a smile. He extended his arm toward Daniel and squeezed his hand. "Nice to meet you."

"The pleasure is all mine."

Dr. Cooper proceeded to introduce a man who was at

least six foot tall, with messy blond hair and a surfer look, which contrasted with his lab coat and formal attire.

"This is Dr. Jerry Shoop. He has been with me for five years. He will be your manager throughout your stay here. So you are in good hands."

"Welcome to the team, Mr. Spence. Looking forward to working with you," he said with a smile as they shook hands.

"Thank you. Likewise." Daniel returned his best PR smile.

Dr. Cooper turned and gestured to Kelly. "I believe you met Mrs. Marshall. She received the Olivia Sponsorship las year and has been with us almost ten months."

They shook hands across the table. "Nice to see you again, Mrs. Marshall," he said with a smile, looking at her prominent hazel eyes.

"Welcome back, Mr. Spence."

Dr. Cooper took out his silver pocket watch and glanced at it. "All right, thank you, everyone. You can get back to work now. It is already past six thirty, so we can finish our discussion tomorrow. Dr. Shoop, I'll meet you in a second." He turned to Daniel. "Mr. Spence, Dr. Cowen will now give you a small tour of our facility, but before you go, I have something for you."

Kelly and Dr. Shoop left the room, and Dr. Cowen stood next to Daniel. Dr. Cooper reached inside one of his lab coat pockets and took out a small book with a pen.

"This is your dream journal, Mr. Spence. It is imperative that you get in the habit of recording your dreams. There is also a poem on the first page that you should read before going to sleep and right after waking up."

Daniel was a bit thrown off by this. "Of course, consider it done." His puzzled expression must have given him away.

"This is part of our particular methods—in fact, everyone at the institute has one. Don't worry. Everything will make sense in due time. For now, I ask for your trust."

Daniel wanted to ask more, but Dr. Cooper continued. "Are you ready, Dr. Cowen?" he said, looking over Daniel's shoulder.

The man stood near the door with his arms crossed, leaning against the wall.

"Yes," he said, glancing at Daniel and then looking back at Dr. Cooper. "I can meet you around midnight tonight."

"That should work," Dr. Cooper replied. He shifted back to Daniel, who put the small journal and pen in his front pocket of his jacket.

"After dinner you'll meet with Dr. Shoop here and go over your first set of duties. I'll see you soon."

"Thank you, Dr. Cooper."

They shook hands, and the old man left the room.

Daniel followed Dr. Cowen out and down the hallway.

"The room we just left is the meeting room," Dr. Cowen said. "It is connected to the computer lab, which you can also access through this door." He pointed to a second white door to his left.

"Interesting. What type of computers do you guys use?" Daniel asked as he walked behind him.

"Mackintosh II's," responded Dr. Cowen without looking back.

"Oh nice. Do you guys spend a lot of time there, working together?"

"A good amount."

Daniel expected a follow-up question, but it never came. They passed the cafeteria, a large space with skylights that was open 24/7. It could probably hold one hundred people or even more.

"How many people work at the institute?" Daniel asked.

"I don't know the exact number," Dr. Cowen replied, appearing a bit irritated as he rushed toward the elevator. "The institute used to be packed back in the seventies, running at full capacity, but those were the golden days."

Daniel wondered what happened after that, but before he could ask, Dr. Cowen spoke again.

"So, the next thing you need to learn is our color coding."

The elevator opened and they walked in. Dr. Cowen pushed the button for Level 2 and to Daniel's surprise, the elevator started going downwards. He had the strange feeling of going into a deep burrow.

"Every experimental room has a light indicator that lights up with a different color depending on the activity of the room."

The elevator stopped, and they stepped out. Dr. Cowen pointed to the right. Around twenty-five feet away, Daniel could see three different doors, one on each side. They all had red lights on above them.

"The green color means you can access that door, the yellow color means there is an ongoing experiment, and the red color mean it's a restricted area."

"I see." Daniel turned around and noticed the hallway was shorter on that end, with two doors on each side. One was a gate with metal bars which had a green light, and the other one was a small door with a blue light.

"So, we have green, yellow, and red lights, but what about that blue one? An even higher level of security? Nuclear experimentation?" said Daniel, smiling. He wanted to break the ice.

"That's the janitor's closet," Dr. Cowen responded, annoyance in his voice.

"Oh, of course," Daniel said quietly.

"Now, the one next to it, though, is the library. That's where we keep records from all our experiments, as well as any books or support Dr. Cooper might think fits our research." He grabbed a key card from his pocket and gave it to Daniel.

"That is your key card. I assume you know how to use one."

Daniel remained silent and felt his ears getting hot.

His guide swiped them in and turned the lights on. The library went forty feet in each direction, with higher ceilings than the one on the stretch hallway. All this helped Daniel to not feel like a rodent anymore. The room had bookshelves from floor to ceiling all the way across.

"Each unit has five shelves. Usually the records of an experiment can take two to three shelves, depending on its complexity and duration." Dr. Cowen sounded proud, as if he were talking about a trophy or a diploma he'd earned.

"That is a lot of information," Daniel said in awe.

Dr. Cowen turned to look at Daniel for the first time since the tour started. "Indeed, we used to have a supervisor for all of this. Not anymore. Now you can see that each level on each stack is closed and properly labeled. You can use your card to open the one you need. But your access will be limited to the information that is relevant to you."

Dr. Cowen pointed to the far left of the library, where there was a counter and a door.

"That one there is our resource room. If you need anything specific for an experiment, they will probably have it. If they don't, they can order it for you. They're pretty helpful."

"Very efficient," Daniel said as Dr. Cowen left the room.

He stood there for a couple of seconds, feeling a heavy weight in the air. It was as if all the memories of The Cooper Institute were cluttered there in the stacks, to be forgotten.

"Mr. Spence?" His tour guide waited by the door with a slightly annoyed expression, ready to turn off the light. Daniel turned around and followed him.

"How many of those experiments have you worked on, Dr. Cowen?" he asked as they stepped out and went toward the elevator.

"A good few," he replied, a bit of nostalgia in his voice. "I like to think I've left a positive footprint there so far. It has been quite the journey."

"What do the experiments consist of mostly? I could not tell from my interview. I mean, I understood where we are going, our goal, but not how we would get there." Daniel knew that asking Mr. Grumpy all of this would be a long shot, but after seeing all the information, he could not resist.

Dr. Cowen's response was quick and sharp. "You will learn that in good time...or not. Dr. Cooper decides how much information is filtered into each researcher. But he always has the bigger picture in his head. I've seen interns who only do paperwork and interns who have helped us directly in our experiments. So you just have got to prove your worth."

Daniel wanted to respond, but Dr. Cowen continued. "We'll go to your room now. The rest of this floor consists of experiment rooms. Same thing with Level Three, as you can see, toward the other side of the hallway. But that's not part of our little tour."

He called the elevator, and the doors opened instantly. Dr. Cowen pressed the button for the fourth floor. Daniel looked down the hallway and saw the red indicator light on top of each door.

"Are you coming in?"

"Oh yes, sorry about that." Daniel went in and noticed there were nine floors.

"You'll get to know the different types of experiments when or if you get assigned to them," Dr. Cowen said. "I've been here for ten years and still don't know what's behind some of those doors."

But Daniel's mind had wandered off. He felt a certain discomfort as the elevator descended. Like a child who's told not to go into a room, all he wanted was to go in that room, whatever monster may be waiting on the other side of the door. Except in his case he was in a house full of those rooms.

"Doesn't that bother you?" The words escaped his mouth before he could hold them back.

"Pardon me?"

"Sorry, I was thinking out loud. I'm just very curious to know what's happening here. After all, this is The Cooper Institute. Every door can open on to a new discovery." His voice was cautious.

Dr. Cowen cleared his throat. "Well, of course some

of those rooms are not in use anymore—most of them, actually." The elevator doors opened, and they stepped out. "Anyway, I don't have to explain to you how or why things work here the way they do," he snapped as they walked faster and stopped in front of a Room 271.

"Your card key is also your room key, so don't lose it, or you will be sleeping outside. It is"—he checked his watch—"seven fifteen right now. Our meal starts at seven thirty. Dr. Shoop will meet you at the computer lab around eight. Any last questions?"

"I think that's all. Thanks you for your time, Dr. Cowen," Daniel said, grinning.

"Of course," Dr. Cowen replied with a bored expression on his face. He walked away.

Cocky idiot.

Daniel went into his new room. He dropped his backpack to the floor and lay on the bed, faceup, staring at the fluorescent lamps. He looked around the simple, college dorm–like room and wasn't impressed. It had no windows, an old wooden closet, and a slight smell that he'd never smelled before—the smell of something that had been locked in there for a while maybe. He assumed he would get used to it.

Daniel used this time to collect his thoughts. He had accepted a job at one of the most renowned institutes in United States and the world; he did this to prove to (*his father*) himself that he could and would make an impact on his own. It was clear to him that The Cooper Institute had seen better days. He deduced that from the size of the team versus the capacity of the building.

Now, neither Dr. Cooper nor Dr. Cowen had told him the details or even the main objective of the overall research, but based on his interview with Dr. Cooper, he knew it was related to the mind and that the government was involved. But what did that even mean? How can you test the mind? And more importantly, what was the use of it? Why was the government interested in something so—let's say—philosophical?

All these questions flew around his head for a moment. After analyzing all the information he learned on the tour and during his interview—which was not much, really—he came to the conclusion that he was still in the dark. He'd need to go through his first experiment before he could figure out anything else. Disappointed, he decided to take a quick shower. As he took his jacket off, he felt the small journal Dr. Cooper gave him upon his arrival earlier, another piece of this puzzle. His curiosity and hopes spiked again. He took it out of his pocket and inspected it. It was made out of smooth black leather. Daniel opened it and read the poem on the first page.

"A Dream within a Dream,"
a poem by Edgar Allan Poe

Take this kiss upon the brow!
And, in parting from you now,
Thus much let me avow—
You are not wrong, who deem
That my days have been a dream;
Yet if hope has flown away

In a night, or in a day,
In a vision, or in none,
Is it therefore the less gone?
All that we see or seem
Is but a dream within a dream.

I stand amid the roar
Of a surf-tormented shore,
And I hold within my hand
Grains of the golden sand—
How few! yet how they creep
Through my fingers to the deep,
While I weep—while I weep!
O God! can I not grasp
Them with a tighter clasp?
O God! can I not save
One from the pitiless wave?
Is all that we see or seem
But a dream within a dream?

He finished the poem and remained quiet for a bit. Instead of answers, the poem generated more questions, the loudest one being:

What the hell is this place?

CHAPTER 4

"HELLO, DR. SHOOP. Dr. Cooper said you would show me my first experiment."

The computer lab had ten cubicles facing the walls. They were placed on the perimeter of the room, with a large printer on the opposite corner from the door. Dr. Shoop sat in the cubicle closest to the door. He was focused on his computer when Daniel approached him. He turned and stared at Daniel for a couple of seconds, like he was coming back from whatever place he was in his research and processing what Daniel said. Then he rolled back in his chair and stood up.

"Right. How are you, Mr. Spence? Did you have dinner already?"

His voice was relaxed and casual, and when he spoke, a small smirk appeared on his face.

"Yes, I grabbed a quick bite before joining you. Everything is good. Just settled into my new room," Daniel replied, feeling a bit more relaxed.

"Excellent. Well, let's get going."

Dr. Shoop led Daniel to the door, and they walked side

by side toward the elevator. On their way, they ended up talking about football and if the New England Patriots had a shot this year.

"Pretty sure they are not going to make it this season, not even to the wildcard game like last year," Dr. Shoop said while he swiped the door with "2A" on it.

Daniel wanted to argue that Bledsoe was still pretty young but his passing was great and he had a promising career. Daniel strongly believed that 1995 would finally be their year. He wanted to remind Dr. Shoop of that epic comeback against the Minnesota Vikings in the second half for a final score of 26–20. But as soon as Dr. Shoop opened the door and he peeked inside, words failed him.

Daniel stood by the door, horrified by what he was seeing. He felt goose bumps on the back of his neck as he walked in with caution and petrified wonder. An old man—in his seventies probably—lay in a reclining medical chair. He was skin and bone. His hospital gown dangled from him like it would from a coat hanger. His eyes were closed, giving the impression he was in a deep sleep. He had a tube coming out of his half-open mouth connected to a mechanical ventilator. There was also an electrocardiograph monitoring the activity of his heart. An oximeter on his finger monitored his pulse and the oxygen level in his blood, and an IV went to his left arm. He would have looked like a patient in a coma or with terminal cancer if it wasn't for the metallic cables that penetrated his bald scalp. It looked like he had tentacles coming from his head going in different directions. Daniel followed them and saw how they all ended up penetrating the ceiling, going into God knew what or where. He reached the end of the reclining chair slowly, as if any abrupt movement might wake up the old man.

"I know it can be a bit shocking, Mr. Spence. It certainly is a gruesome sight," Dr. Shoop said from the other end of the reclining chair. "But everything will make sense in a minute. Allow me to explain."

Daniel snapped back from his thoughts and looked at Dr. Shoop. "I'm all ears," he said with a smile as he put his sweaty hands in his lab coat pockets.

"Good man. This is subject 2-47B. He has been in what we call a state of electrocerebral inactivity, or ECI. His electroencephalogram, better known as an EEG, shows no cortical activity above two microvolts, so there is no brain activity. This also applies to his brain stem reflexes. In a nutshell, he is brain-dead. Now, you are probably wondering about the cables." Dr. Shoop nodded toward them.

"They did catch my attention, yes," Daniel said, trying to sound casual. He noticed that behind him was a desk with a computer and a screen.

"This is the first DSD ever created, which stands for 'Dream Screen Display.' The name is pretty self-explanatory. Those cables are connected to the brain. They record the electrical impulses and translate the dreams the subject has onto that screen next to the computer."

"I never knew computers could do all that." Daniel's eyes widened with surprise, yet there was some distrust in his voice.

Dr. Shoop smiled. "Welcome to The Cooper Institute." He gestured toward the screen at the desk. "The objective of this experiment is to find out if someone with irreparable brain damage can dream. If that is the case, it will prove—"

"That the dream is happening somewhere else besides the brain," Daniel filled in.

"Precisely," Dr. Shoop said with a broad smile, looking at Daniel.

"But then, if it's not happening in the brain, where would it be?" Daniel said, crossing his arms. "And how do we know that what we are seeing, if we even see anything, is accurate and an actual dream?"

"Good questions. To answer your second one, we have proven through different methods that the DSD works and is able to display dreams—"

"What methods?" Daniel said eagerly.

Dr. Shoop briefly closed his eyes and took a deep breath. "I'm afraid I can't tell you that now. Just rest assured that this works. You will find out soon enough, so I'm going to ask for a bit of trust here."

Daniel wanted to argue, but he also knew his limits. Dr. Shoop was so far the nicest person at The Cooper Institute and a potential mentor as his manager. So for once he silenced his curiosity and just said, "All right, you have my trust."

"Glad we understand each other," Dr. Shoop said with a smirk and winked. "Now, to answer your first and more important question—Where would the dreams happen if not in the brain?—that is for us to find out here, don't you think? But before the baby can walk, he needs to learn how to crawl. Before he can crawl, he needs to see. When they are born, babies have very primitive senses. It can take up to a year for them to develop full sight. We are at the birth stage, Mr. Spence. We want to learn whether the baby is premature and needs to be put back in an incubator, or if he is ready to see. Do you understand what I mean?"

Daniel understood all right. He knew damn well what Dr. Shoop meant. This was a test. He needed to find the answer here before they would allow him to see further experiments and what was really happening at the institute. And if he failed…Well, his future would involve a lot of paperwork.

"Loud and clear," Daniel said, looking into Dr. Shoop's brown eyes.

"Good. Now, what you have to do is stimulate our subjects in different ways in order to see if that triggers a response." He turned around and approached the DSD screen. Dr. Shoop reached for the bottom of it and turned it on. After a couple of seconds, a black glow appeared on the screen. "This is the neutral stage of the DSD. If any sort of dream pulses happen, it'll manifest here," he said, knocking on the upper side of the monitor, and then he pointed at the CPU under the table. "And it'll be saved in the computer's CPU. There is a folder on the desktop called DSD. So even if something happens while you are not here, a message should pop up and warn you. If there is any sort of activity, even for a fraction of a second, it'll be there."

"Got it. What exactly would be displayed?" Daniel asked as he inspected the monitor closely.

"It can be a very clear dream, with sequential images and even sounds, it can be random images, and it can even be just abstract figures and colors. For our purposes, we just want the reaction. Now, you can stimulate the subject's senses any way you want. You can get any materials you might need downstairs in the library. Any questions?"

"Not really. I just need to monitor and stimulate the subject until I get a reaction on the DSD—sounds pretty simple," Daniel answered, looking back at the old man's face and feeling remorse. This whole time they had been talking about him like he was a lab rat.

"Then I think we are good to go. We have a control subject next door, in 2-48B. I'll monitor her. She is basically in the same conditions as our friend here. Of course, I won't apply any stimuli. That way, we have a reference point." He put his hand on Daniel's shoulder. "That's all. If you need anything, I'll be next door."

"Sounds good, Dr. Shoop. I think I can take it from here," Daniel said with confidence.

Dr. Shoop patted his shoulder twice and walked out.

As soon as the door shut, Daniel started working. He found notebooks, pens, calculators, and other materials in the drawer. He sat down and, just before he started, noticed the old man's head and torso to his left. His heart jumped before he realized it was his reflection in a small mirror to the left of his desk. He assumed the mirror was there so he could keep an eye on the subject while working, but then wondered why, if that was the case, not just turn the desk? Definitely odd, but not enough to distract him from his duties.

For the next hour, he laid out a detailed plan of action to approach his experiment. He divided it into tasks and milestones, described how he'd stimulate each sense separately and at different intensities. Around an hour later, he was done and ready, with a defined schedule and step-by-step plan. That was always Daniel's way. No matter how easy or hard something looked, he always broke it down into steps and developed a detailed plan of action. The approach never failed him in college or grad school or even with his father, so it would not fail him now.

He wrote down a list of materials and stood up with the intention of leaving the room, but something stopped him. The constant sound of air flowing in and out of the mechanical ventilator; the electrocardiograph making a high-pitch beeping sound with each heartbeat. More than background noise, it was a reminder: Daniel was not alone here. He walked toward the door, only to stop as he turned the handle. He looked back at the subject; he had a clear view of the old man's profile and all the metallic cables coming from him. Daniel felt something in his chest. Was it remorse? Pity? Maybe both. His focus shifted from the back of the old man's head to the ventilator. For a second, he looked at its cable, connected to the outlet in the wall, before pushing his thoughts away and leaving the room.

The lights in the library came on by section as Daniel walked in, feeling the same gloomy loneliness he felt when he did his tour. He went toward the half-glass door under the "Resource Room" sign and spoke through the five holes.

"Hello?"

Ten seconds later, a lady probably in her midfifties rolled over in her office chair. Her hair was blond and short, she was a bit overweight, and she had a decent-sized mole on her left cheek. She was chewing gum in a monotonous way. Her blue eyes met Daniel's.

"Can I help you?" Her voice was also monotonous.

"Hello, I'm Daniel Spence. I need some materials for my experiment."

"Credentials please." Her gum chewing produced extra saliva in her mouth, which she spit every time she said a word.

"You mean my key?"

"Do you have anything else?"

"No."

She did not respond; instead, she stared with bored eyes. Daniel understood and slid his key under the glass opening below the five holes.

You must be fun at parties.

She grabbed the key and rolled out of view. Shortly after, she rolled back. Her expression, or lack of one, remained.

"List."

Daniel took it out and slid it through the lower opening. She grabbed it, stood up, and walked away.

Daniel stood there for a good chunk of time, checking out the huge space. He rested his back against the wall next to the door, feeling the extra hours he had been awake. He did not know what time it was, but he could guess it was past midnight. His body was feeling heavier by the second, and his eyes were slowly closing. He struggled for a bit, especially considering the baleful feel of the lonely space.

Not two minutes later, as he was swimming in a sea of drowsiness, all the lights turned off. If it wasn't for the white light coming out of the "Resources" room, he would've been completely submerged in darkness. Surprised, he just stood there, waiting for something to happen, without really knowing what to expect. His senses tuned in: his eyes tried to find movement in the dark, and his ears sharpened to any sound.

The silence resonated in the large room. Then something made his skin crawl. Steps—a sound as common as that in a setting like this—disturbed the ordinariness. They sounded far away in the darkness and were moving at a steady pace. Daniel just listened, with his mouth half-open. He thought of leaving, but there wasn't a clear path to walk out, to escape; he was cornered. The steps were getting louder, closer, their pace still steady.

Daniel tried to speak but couldn't. A dense ball of fear was stuck in his throat as he closed his fists, breathing heavily. Very little of the light hitting the floor in front of him bounced back up, but it was enough to reveal a silhouette. It was the shape of a tall person, but any other details were impossible to discern.

Every second felt like an eternity, and finally, words struggled out of Daniel's dry mouth.

"Who's there?" His voice came out with authority, and the echo resonated around the walls and stacks of the library.

No response. Daniel felt a chilling cold slide down his spine as his heartbeat pressed his chest. Two white marbles suddenly appeared in the silhouette's head. His eyes met them, and he was petrified. The silhouette took a couple more steps, and now Daniel could see its feet, with pale skin and maybe bulging green veins—he wasn't sure.

A loud, fast rapping noise coming from the glass door to his left made Daniel jump.

"You still there? I got your materials," the monotonous voice said through the holes of the glass.

Daniel looked back to where the two marbles had been, but they were gone. Still breathing heavily, he stood back in front of the glass door. The woman was standing there with a cardboard box.

"Yes…Thank you." His voice was a bit shaky, and he could feel drops of sweat running down his forehead. "Do you know why the lights went out?"

The woman unbolted an opening and slid the box out, her expression not changing one bit. "What are you talking about?"

Daniel turned around and realized all the lights were on again and everything seemed fine. Regardless, he was sure of what he saw.

"Is this your first week here?" The lady now had a touch of interest in her voice, even though her chewing-gum habit suggested the opposite.

Daniel looked back, realizing how dumb he must look. He cleared his throat and leaned down to pick up the box. "First day, actually." He gave a fake smile.

"Ah…I've seen this before. Don't worry, I've worked here for longer than you have been alive probably. Most likely you just fell asleep and didn't notice it. The grave-yard shift can be tough on some people, especially the first couple of days."

This calmed Daniel down, and suddenly the woman did not seem like a big asshole anymore.

"Yeah, I probably just fell asleep. Well, thank you for the materials."

"Just return them in a week. Or if you need them for a longer period, make an extension request."

With that, she rolled out of view, and Daniel walked out. At the door, he turned the light off and could not stop himself from looking back at the empty darkness, wondering.

CHAPTER 5

THREE DAYS LATER, toward the end of the night, an exhausted Daniel stared at the ceiling, lost in thought. The graveyard shift and the loneliness had not made any of this easy. He assumed it was just a matter of time before he'd adjust to the new job, but the truth was that he was struggling. He hadn't crossed paths with Dr. Shoop or any of the other research partners. Hell, even Dr. Cowen seemed like appealing company right now. But what was probably affecting Daniel the most was the lack of results from his experiment. From six in the evening until eight or nine in the morning, he would follow his detailed steps but get no answers.

Then, as often happened when he was swimming in his thoughts, the voice of Dr. Cooper came back to him: "Everything you think you know about the human mind is a lie." That statement had haunted him since his interview. He knew he'd been referring to dreams, because of his experiment and because of the weird task with the dream journal. Daniel also deducted, after thinking back to his conversation with Dr. Shoop, that this first experiment was a sort of test for him: the more results he could deliver, the more he would be told. And he could not forget the chilling library (*incident*) dream he had. Although he had to dismiss it as a dream, the vividness of the event was still fresh in his mind, and that made the whole space more bizarre. But none of these things really came close to explaining something as complicated as the human mind and its connection to the brain.

Added to all of this, Daniel developed a feeling of guilt as he continued to experiment with the old man. He felt like he was violating his privacy and integrity, taking advantage of him and his situation. Being in a room with someone who was there but not present was an oddly familiar feeling for Daniel. While he was seated in a sort of trance, a flood of memories hit his brain, and he was back sixteen years to that somber dinner with his father. The two of them were sitting at the dining table, not really talking but not really eating, either. His father would just take sips of his soup from time to time, his gaze fixed on the table, a lost look on his face.

The cold fall wind hitting the windows had nothing to do with the coldness Daniel, then a nine-year-old, felt. He ate his dinner quietly, despair developing in his heart and stomach. The silence in the room, denser than water, pressured the little boy's chest, making it hard to breathe, until he could not handle it anymore. So, with a mixture of bravery and fear, he looked up at his father.

"Dad?"

His sweet child's voice landed in Robert Spence's ears. No response came.

Daniel looked back down. Small, bitter tears accumulated in his eyes and made his vision glossy. He tried to hold them back, but one slid out and slid down his nose and into his soup. That was the moment Daniel Spence realized he was alone. His father was physically there, but the loving father of two children with a beautiful wife had gone the moment Katherine Spence swallowed those damn pills for depression.

A knock on the door brought Daniel back.

"Come in," Daniel said, wiping one eye with his lab coat.

Dr. Shoop walked in with his relaxed vibe. "Good morning, Mr. Spence. Wanted to pay you a visit and check how things are going."

"Hello, Dr. Shoop. Things are going okay," Daniel responded while shifting his gaze from Dr. Shoop to the subject.

"Could be better, huh?" Dr. Shoop said as he leaned next to Daniel and looked back at the subject too. "Don't feel discouraged, it's a though experiment."

Daniel appreciated his words but wished he wasn't having this conversation. "Yeah, it is...I just wish I had some sort of lead I could follow. As of now, I'm in the same spot I was last time you saw me, three days ago."

Dr. Shoop turned around and looked down at the desk. "Why don't you walk me through your approach so far? I've found that explaining something to someone else helps when I'm stuck."

Daniel looked at him with gratitude and felt a bit of shame, but he needed all the help he could get.

"All right, if you have the time to spare, I could use a second opinion," Daniel responded, turning around and starting to go through his notes.

For the next hour or so, Daniel explained in detail his approach and how nothing had happened so far. Dr. Shoop listened carefully, and once Daniel was done, he gave him his diagnosis.

"The reason why I think this is taking so long is because you are testing each sense separately. Again, it is not a bad approach—in fact, it can tell us more in the end. You are off to a good start."

His words came as a relief to Daniel. He leaned against the desk. "Dr. Shoop, do you know why Dr. Cooper assigned me this experiment?"

His manager leaned back next to him again and crossed his arms. Now they were both facing the subject. His answer was accompanied by a smirk. "He is a fascinating man, Dr. Cooper. I wish I knew the answer to that question myself. He is the mastermind behind everything that has been happening here. He sees the big picture, then divides it into pieces and spreads it around his researchers. But even between us we cannot put everything together, because he holds on to crucial things. So we just have to trust him." This last sentence came with a bit of bitterness both in his voice and expression as he looked at the subject.

Daniel took a deep breath. "That must be frustrating, working on something for a long time without really knowing where it's going, not really having an end goal." Dr. Shoop remained quiet, so Daniel carried on. "If you don't mind me asking, you did not say this explicitly before, but based on our previous conversation, is this experiment a sort of test? That whole analogy with the baby being able to see before he can crawl had me thinking—"

Dr. Shoop laughed, interrupting him. "I must say, Mr.

Spence, your imagination is quite fascinating. I think I know what is happening. When was the last time you stepped outside?" He smiled and exchanged looks with Daniel, who felt a bit ashamed now.

He thought about it for a bit and was surprised by the answer. "I haven't stepped outside since I first got here."

"Well, that explains it. Why don't you take a fifteen-minute break, step out the building, stretch out, smoke, or something? I'll stay here and monitor the subject."

"Are you sure?"

Dr. Shoop patted his back. "Of course. You have fifteen minutes. Now, go before you go all loon here."

Daniel stepped outside for the first time in more than seventy-two hours. It was still dark out, but morning would come any moment now. The soft, cool wind of early morning brushed his face, and he took a deep breath. The air filled his lungs, and he stretched, relaxing for the first time in a while. Daniel then realized how much he had missed being outside. He never expected the internship to be so challenging, but then again, most people take the pleasures of life for granted until they are taken away.

"Taking a small break, I suppose?" a female voice said from behind. A second later, Kelly Marshall, the other intern, stood next to him.

"Oh, yes I am. I haven't been outside since I first moved in, so Dr. Shoop told me to do it," Daniel said, placing his hands behind his back.

"Yeah, I figured. Happened the same way to me too. Except my manager is Dr. Cowen, and let's just say he is not a big fan of breaks. I didn't know I could step out for one until Dr. Cooper saw me and told me late one morning. I must have looked terrible for him to notice."

She laughed, and Daniel smiled.

"It's hard to remember when you are so focused and also when you are three levels underground," Daniel said. "You sort of start to get used to it. Next thing you know, we'll have black eyes and tails—we'll be like rodents. Or worse, we might end up looking like Dr. Cowen," he added, and felt relieved when she laughed hard and was not offended by a joke about her manager.

"Care if I smoke?" she said, pulling out a box of Camels.

"Care? I'd love to join, if you don't mind sparing one."

She smiled and offered her pack, which was almost full. Daniel saw that one of the cigarettes was placed upside down, with the white portion pointing up.

Ah, the lucky one. The one that shall be smoked last.

He took another one and lit it. He took a big puff and felt how his years as a smoker came back. What was it people always said? Once a smoker always a smoker.

"It's weird. No one else in the institute smokes. I think it's actually healthier in my case, because it forces me to come outside," Kelly said while looking up at the sky. Daniel followed her gaze and saw the beautiful starry night.

"Yeah, I agree. I used to be a heavy smoker, but now I just do it occasionally."

They both stood there quietly, taking drags and enjoying the calm of the wind. Although the break was short, Daniel felt at peace. His thoughts about the experiment and questions about the institute slowly crawled back into his head.

"So, you have been at the institute for six months, correct? What do you think of it so far?"

Kelly took a puff and looked at Daniel. "It's been interesting. There are many things to learn from this place, but you have to be very patient."

"I see. Yeah, from secretary last winter to a researcher in the summer. That's what I call perseverance," he teased her with a smile.

"Ha, we have a funny one over here. Actually, I was just covering for Nancy. The poor woman was sick and was gone for almost two weeks. She is very old. I think she is the oldest person working at the institute. If it wasn't for my initiative, all those monkeys inside would have gone mad." Daniel smiled as he took another drag. Kelly took a second cigarette and lit it up. She offered the pack to Daniel, but he waved it back. He knew his limits. "Besides, research has shown that women are more suited to do multiple jobs. Men tend to get…confused when it comes down to splitting tasks."

Daniel laughed hard at this. A woman with an attitude; something hard to find these days. "So, you probably had a closer look at all the logistics happening here." Now Daniel saw a chance, and even though he enjoyed the peace he had two minutes ago, his curiosity got the better of him.

Kelly looked at him with a puzzled expression. "Yes, a little bit. Why do you ask?"

"Oh I'm just, you know, asking around," Daniel said as he shrugged and avoided Kelly's gaze by looking up at the night sky. "I want to understand what is really going on here, you know? Get more familiar with the place."

"I have a little suggestion for you, Mr. Spence," she snapped. "If I were you Sherlock, I would focus on the research and drop the detective role."

Daniel felt how his frustration from the past couple of days came out in a loud tone. "Why is everyone here—?"

"Quiet your voice, Mr. Spence," Kelly said through gritted teeth. "What we are doing here is bigger than you could even imagine. So if you can suck it up and focus on getting results, you might understand one day." She took one last drag and dropped her cigarette. "Thanks for the good company," she said saltily, then turned around and walked back in.

Daniel stood there, mad at himself. It wasn't in him to lose composure like that. He knew he lost an opportunity to start a good relationship with his coworker. But his urge to know what was going on got the better of him; now he just hoped the damage could be fixed.

He looked down at the still-lit cigarette on the ground, stepped on it, swiveling his foot multiple times, and went back inside.

CHAPTER 6

Daniel sighed as he clumsily placed the headphones on the subject. They lay awkwardly across his forehead because of all the cables coming out of his scalp. As the music went on, he opened one of the subject's eyelids and stuck it open with clear tape. He shone a flashlight directly at the eye, switching it on and off. As expected, his pupil stayed dilated and fixed. Daniel grabbed a pin and slowly pressed the point against the subject's forearm. He was close enough to smell the old man's particular odor. Daniel assumed someone washed him every so often; otherwise, he'd be rotting in that bed.

"Oh my dear friend, we sure have shared some quality time the last couple of days," Daniel said as if expecting a response.

After an hour or so, he took off the headphones, closed the eyelid—he'd periodically open and close it to make sure the eye would stay moist—and stopped pinching him. He went back to his desk and wrote down the results. Daniel sighed deeply, placed his elbows on the table, and rested his face in his palms. Nothing was working, and the experiment was as tedious as it could get. He stayed like that for a while, submerged in his thoughts, which were oscillating between speculation about this place, the ethical dimension of the experiment, and doubt about what he was doing overall. Then an image of his dad appeared, and Daniel heard the bastard lecturing him in his professorial voice—"You finally have one job that is not in my office, and you come back crawling after a week"—with a disapproving look on his face, the one Daniel was so used to seeing. "I can't say I'm surprised. I'll see you in my office first thing in the morning. You are not going to just lay around doing nothing for the rest of the summer." Daniel felt anger crawling up his body and heat in his ears. He could not stand the picture of his disapproving father, so he opened his eyes and lifted his head back up.

Daniel was staring at the black screen of the DSD when he first felt it. A very slight but cold breeze brushed his neck, raising every single hair. He massaged it briefly.

They want me to find something, I'm sure of it. It's like they already know the answer. They just want to see if I can find it too.

But there was something bothering Daniel Spence that night. He was not sure when the feeling started, but it increased as time progressed. It was like that feeling you get when you are not alone in a space. Like walking down a dark alley and constantly turning around because something inside is telling you someone is following. Or being in the darker corners of a huge college library and feeling something strange and thick both in your chest and on the back of your neck: the feeling of being watched.

"What we are doing here is bigger than you could even

imagine. So if you can suck it up and focus on getting results, you might understand one day."

A similar feeling slowly grew inside Daniel, and that was when he realized he had not turned around and checked on the subject for a while: How long? He didn't know, but it seemed like hours.

Everything you think you know about the human mind is a lie.

Then, giving up to this strange feeling, he turned.

The room was empty—except for the subject, of course. Everything seemed normal, so he turned back.

Silly. The only other person in this room is the subject, and I am sure he has his eyes closed. I am sure…

Daniel felt the need to check on the subject, but he ignored the impulse. He laughed out loud.

"I would have seen you looking at me before."

His voice was louder than usual. Yet he still felt that unsettling fear. It kept growing and growing inside. He looked down at the pointless mirror, expecting to see the old man's head and shoulder like he had for the past couple of days. What he saw was even stranger: the mirror wasn't working. He rubbed it, thinking it might be foggy, but it was useless. It was as if it wasn't a mirror anymore but a dull surface.

What the hell?

Daniel grabbed it and rubbed it harder this time, using his lab coat. There was something very wrong, but he wasn't sure what. He could just feel it in his bones. Another soft, cold breeze hit the back of his neck, and this time his whole body froze. Something was watching him, something was there, but what? There was only one way to find out.

Daniel turned around slowly and was petrified by what he saw. He sat there, dazed, as he exchanged a look with the subject. The old man shifted his head toward Daniel slowly—thanks to all the cables encrusted in his skull. Croaky noises came from the old man's throat as he tried to speak but couldn't because of the tube coming from his mouth. He raised an emaciated hand with loose skin and leaned forward. Then his eyes twisted inwards, as if he were looking inside his own skull, leaving two white marbles instead. A crooked smile formed at the corners of his mouth, and the croaky noises coming from his throat were now intermittent.

He was laughing.

CHAPTER 7

Daniel jumped back up, sweating and gasping for air. He was disoriented and dizzy, but on impulse he checked the mirror on his desk. It showed the old man's face and upper body, like it always did. He turned around and found the subject lying there, eyes closed. He cleaned the cold sweat off his forehead as he tried to calm down and recollect what just happened. In his dream, although at first scary, the subject's face was one of a beggar. Like he was asking for some sort of mercy. Yes, he was sure; he saw the suffering in the man's face. At least before his eyes changed and that creepy smile was drawn on his lips.

Regardless, he could not avoid thinking back to his nightmare the first day at the library. He had not thought about it much since he wrote about it in his journal; it was as if by writing about it, part of its vividness was taken away. But now he felt something very similar, something rather… bizarre.

He turned back to his desk when something caught his attention. His monitor displayed a pop-up message. It said there was new content in the DSD folder. Around twenty different images had been created. Daniel looked at their times, and they were all generated between 3:43 a.m. and 3:57 a.m. Exactly three minutes ago.

Twenty images produced in the span of thirteen minutes without stimuli.

He opened the first image and was puzzled by what he saw. A very light, vertical gray line, sort of like a waft of smoke on a white background. He scrolled through the rest of the images and found the same effect expressed in different ways. Sometimes the line was shorter and diagonal, and then that same diagonal line would be mirrored in the next image. Other times there would be just a very short horizontal line, and so on. Daniel sat back, puzzled, looking at all of them. Dr. Shoop did mention the images could be very abstract, but the waft of light-gray smoke was barely noticeable.

Daniel printed them out and laid them on his desk. Each image was in order, with a Post-it note giving the time it was produced. He stared at them for more than an hour, knowing that he could just show Dr. Cooper and Dr. Shoop his results and they would probably be pleased. After all, they just asked for a reaction, not the analysis of that reaction. Yes, it would please them, but it did not please Daniel Spence.

You can call it stubbornness, but when something got in Daniel's head, he would not stop until he found an answer. This started at an early age, in middle school. In biology class, they were studying the nervous system, specifically the electrical impulses from one neuron to another. To show his argument, Mr. Handzy, the teacher, referred to the Galvani/Volta debate on animal electricity, from the 1790s. All the students gathered around the lab table for the experiment. The professor utilized one of the most useless beings alive—at least, in Daniel's opinion—a cockroach. He placed the bug in a bottle and administered carbon dioxide to anesthetize the insect. Then he cut off one of its legs and connected two pins to it. Finally, he grabbed two alligator clips, connected them to a battery, then grabbed the other two ends and connected one to one of the pins.

What happened next created a spark in Daniel's head that triggered a massive explosion of questions that needed answers. Mr. Handzy touched the free pin, and the cockroach's leg started moving on its own.

"Uhh! Wow! Cool!" were the reactions of the kids around him. Daniel, on the other hand, remained quiet as multiple questions fired in his brain: What makes us different from them? If cockroaches have nerve impulses, why haven't they developed a more complex nervous system, like humans? In the end, is the human body just a conglomeration of electrical impulses?

But it was a more fundamental question that came out of Daniel's mouth and left both the class and Mr. Handzy speechless:

"Are the thoughts we have also groups of nerve impulses like the ones used by that cockroach to move its leg?"

Indeed, this caught Mr. Handzy off guard. After a bit of hesitation, he responded, "That's a good question, but it does not relate to today's topic, Daniel. We'll cover that later in the semester."

Of course, a class for twelve-year-olds didn't deal with a question that went deep into the concept of the human mind. But the question endured in Daniel's head, and from that moment it grew roots, a strong trunk, and branched out to create one of Daniel's strongest characteristics today: his scientific drive.

For days, the question danced around him, not leaving him alone. Around a week later, and after a lot of hesitation, he asked his father.

Robert Spence was reading the newspaper and drinking black coffee like every Sunday morning. It was his ritual; he was a creature of habit. Daniel approached him slowly and said in a careful voice, "Dad, can I ask you a question?"

"What is it?" his dad replied from behind his newspaper.

"Well, we did this experiment in biology class, and I wanted to know if you knew the answer to a question I had regarding nerve impulses."

His father put the newspaper down and, with a straight face, said, "Yes?"

Daniel proceeded to explain the experiment with a level of detail impressive for a kid his age. After his explanation, he asked, "So, are cockroaches' nerve impulses to move a leg the same ones that generate our thoughts?"

His father put the newspaper down and looked at Daniel.

"That's a very interesting question, Son, but I'll be doing you more harm than good if I answer it. Instead, you should research it yourself and come up with an answer for me in a week. You can go to the library. I can also provide you with resources if you want. If I simply give you the answer, that's all you are going to take out of it." He leaned forward and placed his hand on Daniel's shoulder. "But if you look for the answer yourself, you will learn a lot more. If you always look, Daniel, you'll always learn."

Now here he was again, seeking an answer based on a question only he had.

After an hour or so, something clicked. He realized his initial approach could be wrong and that maybe these were not separate images but parts of one image. After all, they were lines—smoky lines, but lines nonetheless. With some rearrangement, it became obvious that was the case. It was simple to identify the *K*, but harder to identify the other letters. Daniel organized the images by following the order they were produced in and superimposed them, as if the subject was spelling the word rather than saying it. As Daniel finished spelling it, he felt a cold current run from his neck and down his spine. He turned around and looked at the old man with a perplexed expression. The subject was still in his bed like always. Daniel turned back and read it again:

KILL ME

CHAPTER 8

DANIEL WENT UPSTAIRS to Dr. Cooper's office after checking on Dr. Shoop next door and realizing he wasn't there. On his way, he could not help but think about what he just found and what it could mean.

Is his mind trapped in a useless body? Is the subject suffering? Or is it all a coincidence? No, it can't be, but maybe I made a mistake. No, no, you didn't, Spence. The message is clear once you see it.

He knocked gently on Dr. Cooper's door, but no response came from within. Daniel rushed to the computer lab to see if anyone was there and found Kelly Marshall on one of the computers.

"Kelly, would you happen to know where Dr. Shoop or Dr. Cooper are?" Daniel asked quickly.

She turned around in her chair, and Daniel saw a tired but focused look on her face. "I believe they are with Dr. Cowen in the middle of an experiment. Why do you ask?"

Daniel waited a second before answering. After a quick mental check, he concluded there was no risk in sharing information—and, in fact, if he did, he might gain some of her trust back.

"I just made a major discovery, and I need to talk to them."

Kelly's eyes widened. "Were you working with subject 2-47B?"

"How do you know?"

"Because that was my first experiment here too. So, I'm assuming you finally got some abstract images out of the poor man," Kelly said, leaning back in her chair, arms crossed, with a know-it-all expression on her face.

I knew it; this was a test. Worst yet, if Kelly knows, then probably the whole research team knows too.

"I think it's more than just abstract images," Daniel said, and was pleased to see Kelly's cocky expression fade away as quickly as it had appeared.

"What do you mean?" Kelly said in a flat tone, looking at Daniel in disbelief.

"...Yes, Viktor, I'm well aware of..." Dr. Shoop paused and looked at both of them as he walked into the computer lab with Dr. Cowen. "Oh, Mr. Spence, I'm surprised to see you here. I thought we still had a couple of hours before our shift was over."

"Yes, we do, but..." He looked at Dr. Cowen, who was behind Dr. Shoop, giving him a strange look. "I have some results I would like to discuss with you and Dr. Cooper if possible."

Dr. Shoop smiled. "Well, that's wonderful news. Come, follow me. Dr. Cooper should be back in his office by now."

Dr. Cowen moved left, and Daniel could see a harsh

look on his face. "We'll finish our little chat later, Dr. Cowen."

"Indeed we will."

Daniel walked out the room and looked back just once as the door was closing. He saw Kelly looking back at him, but her expression seemed out of place. She looked worried.

"Dr. Cooper," Dr. Shoop said, knocking on the door softly. "I have Mr. Spence with me."

Dr. Cooper's soft voice came from inside: "Please come in."

They both went in and found him at his desk reading a stack of papers neatly organized in front of him.

To Daniel, it seemed as if he hadn't seen him in months. "Good early morning, Dr. Cooper. Sorry for the late unplanned meeting."

"Do not worry about it. Please have a seat," he said, gesturing to the leather chair in front of his desk. "I'll take it from here, Dr. Shoop."

Daniel turned, a bit confused, but only saw the door closing. He thought his meeting would be with both of them.

"So, what did you find, Mr. Spence?"

Daniel turned back. He placed his folder on the desk and took out the images. He handed them over to Dr. Cooper, who inspected them. As he scrolled through, Daniel explained his strategy and what led to these results. Of course, he left out some details of "lesser importance," such as the little nap he took by accident earlier and the odd dream he had. In his mind, they must be a coincidence. Besides, it would not look good to sleep during work hours as an intern.

So he proceeded to explain how he came to the conclusion that the images were all pieces of the same message. He then explained how he combined them and formed the words "Kill me."

Dr. Cooper listened carefully to everything Daniel said and, once he finished, remained quiet for a bit.

"Very impressive, Mr. Spence," he said calmly with a smile. "Your skills of deduction are well above average. That's without mentioning the fact that you pursued an answer that went beyond the results. So what are your conclusions? And don't just think of an answer. Tell me your thought process."

"Let's see…The subject did not had any brain activity, but still the DSD received images, which are proof that the subject experiences some sort of constant dream. I would have argued that the images could just be a glitch in the system, but based on the message, I think that they were produced by the subject." Daniel stopped, thought about what he just said, and quickly added, "But that's impossible unless—"

"Unless there is something beyond the brain." Dr. Cooper completed his sentence, giving Daniel a patient look, and smiled again. He then stood up. "What do you think of the message itself, Mr. Spence?"

"The message?" Daniel looked down and read it again, while the old man went to the cabinet on his left. He knew his answer might cause conflict, but this has been bothering him from the start. "If I may speak freely…"

"Of course," Dr. Cooper said as he looked for something on one of the shelves.

"I believe our subject is in pain. I think that whatever is left of him inside his head is deeply disturbed and feels trapped." Daniel paused and tried to swallow; his mouth was dry. "So, he is begging for a way out, a way to move on maybe. I know my remark might sound strange, even religious, but based on the sort of blunt message he spelled and his current state, that is my conclusion." His voice trembled a little, and he hoped Dr. Cooper didn't catch that. It was as if his guilt was coming out all at once. So many hours alone with the poor man, confined to a set of machines that kept him alive. And after all that, Daniel received a message, a desperate call for help. Why was he feeling this now? Maybe it was because deep inside he knew something was not right.

Dr. Cooper turned around, carrying a folder, and went back to his seat. "I see…Would your perception change if I told you the man we are using is a convicted rapist and murderer?"

He placed the folder on the table and slid it toward Daniel, who grabbed it and checked it out. The first thing he saw was a mug shot of young, good-looking man. It took him a couple of seconds to realize that it was the subject. Speechless, Daniel looked through the photos and newspaper articles while Dr. Cooper went on.

"His name is Alex Mars. He was a serial killer—one of the worst ones, actually. He was incarcerated in the Metropolitan Correctional Center, in Chicago, for the kidnap, rape, torture, and murder of a fourteen-year-old he had in his basement. Later, the FBI discovered links to other missing teenage girls and boys with the same profile around the area. He is a psychopath who never showed any remorse for what he did. There was as big public outcry. People asked for the death penalty, but instead he got a life sentence." The old man sipped from his coffee as Daniel looked at the horrifying images. "I do not know how much you know about jails, but even they have standards. It does not matter if you are a killer or you stole your mother's car, but the one person who is never accepted is a rapist of minors. Our friend Alex would never back down or shut up when he should, so the whole thing exploded about two months after he went to jail. There was a big brawl in the yard. There was blood everywhere, and a guy ended up in a coma." Dr. Cooper leaned forward, giving the impression he was going to share a great secret. "You can imagine how expensive it is to keep someone on life support, and Big Brother was not going to pay for that…So, before they decided to pull the plug and let him 'die due to his critical condition,' I stepped in. I talked to the people financing us and told them the guy could be of great use in our experiments. So instead of 'letting him go,' they announced he died of his wounds and transferred him here."

Daniel was astonished. "How did you…?"

Dr. Cooper leaned back again, resting his back on his chair. "I pulled some strings here and there. The government has great interest in our research, so they are more flexible with us. Even though we are a private institute, we work closely with them and provide them with useful research. It is a convenient relationship. Besides, the man had no family. No one came for him, not even at his trial."

"Why did no one tell me this?" asked Daniel, closing the folder and sliding it back.

"Would the information have changed anything?"

Daniel thought for a moment: Would it have changed his approach? He did not think so, but then again, those images…

"No…But then, why are you telling me this now?"

Dr. Cooper put his hands together, interlacing his fingers. "Very few people at the institute know about this. In fact, only Dr. Shoop and Dr. Cowen also know. That's because when they performed this experiment, they found the images and questioned them. They stopped and took a step back to see what they meant, what all this could really mean."

"So, as I suspected, this was part of a test. One that is given to every new addition to the research team," Daniel pointed out in a calm and confident voice.

"Are you surprised?" Dr. Cooper responded with a grin on his face before continuing with a professorial tone. "You see, Mr. Spence, that was the first experiment that put me on this journey, this odyssey. It is also a great way to demonstrate that there is a separation between the mind and the brain, because that is the basis of everything we do here. But that's just the beginning. Only the worthy ones, the ones that go a step further and manage to see the message behind the images, have the vision that I'm looking for, the sort of passion I need as we move forward."

Daniel remained silent. Even though all this was good news to him, there was something niggling him.

"Dr. Cooper, would you mind if I ask how long Alex has been at the institute?"

For a second, the old man's face showed a puzzled look before going back to its neutral wise expression. "I believe it should be thirteen years by the fall. Why do you ask?"

Daniel took a deep breath and went for it, as he clearly pictured the subject's face in his dream. "I believe we should disconnect him, Dr. Cooper. I believe that his mind, or whatever is trying to reach us through the DSD, is desperately looking for a way out, for final peace."

Dr. Cooper's eyes widened, and there was a smirk on his face. "This is interesting. What makes you think that?" he said, getting closer.

Daniel crossed his arms and responded, keeping his calm. "Nothing, really. Maybe it's not my place to say this, but I find it a bit inhuman to keep someone in that state."

"You are right, Mr. Spence, it is not your place," Dr. Cooper said, leaning back again. "But I understand your concern. Do not worry. Mr. Mars will be allowed to move on soon." He then added in a casual voice, "Did something happen down there? Something out of the ordinary?"

Daniel's neck froze. He looked at those blue eyes, which had been painted by the brush of time. "No, sir, why do you ask?"

"No particular reason. Well, I'm happy to say that your results have exceeded my expectations. I'll transfer you to a different experiment. Since tomorrow is your day off, I'd like to see you at six thirty Sunday in my office to go over some basics."

Daniel stood up. "Sounds great, Dr. Cooper. Looking forward to it."

On his way back, Daniel's head felt heavy, especially his eyelids. He hadn't realized how much this experiment had drained him, so he decided he would clean up his desk tomorrow and head straight to bed.

Once in his room, he found that sleep evaded him. Was it because he was thinking about Dr. Cooper's next experiment? No, he was thinking about that, but there was something else, something deeper. Humans are fascinating creatures. It does not matter how unlikely something is—they will pursue that atypical outcome in their minds. It's like flying on a plane and thinking about how the plane will crash, or swimming in the ocean and expecting a shark to attack. Daniel's dream with Alex Mars in it was most likely a coincidence, given that they had shared almost every second of the past week, but what if it wasn't? What would it mean if it was real? Not only would it mean that the mind exists but also that other people dreaming could project their minds into a sort of common space. And that was the only place Alex Mars could reach him. Of course, there were some flaws in this logic—for one, why was he still so fragile in that space? Why wasn't he normal? If the mind and the brain were separate, then why did he still look as fragile as he did in real life? Then again, he was speculating that it was not just a dream, which was unlikely.

After an hour or so, Daniel sat up. He realized he would not find sleep until he dealt with the problem. He turned on the night lamp and saw his dream journal on the night-stand. After all the events that night, he had completely forgotten about it. Daniel grabbed it and read the poem by Edgar Allan Poe. Then he got his pen and wrote down his dream in detail. He took special care with the description and also wrote about the image that appeared on the DSD while he was dreaming. Five minutes later, he finished and closed the journal again, feeling a lot lighter. He felt as if he had transferred the weight of the events to that journal. He turned the light off, but there was still something bothering him. Not five minutes passed when he turned the light back on and wrote:

To the best of my abilities, I still can't say how much of this dream was just a dream and how much of it was something else. How much of all of this is really just a coincidence.

It seemed redundant at first, but writing that took a weight off his shoulders. Finally, Daniel turned off the night lamp and lay back on his bed. Sleep found him shortly after.

CHAPTER 9

DANIEL SPENCE WOKE up after a deep sleep that Saturday around evening time. No dreams reached him in his sleep, and he was thankful for that. He took a shower, got dressed, and went to clean his desk before eating "breakfast."

He walked into Room 2B intending to just grab his notes and documents, then leave. But he saw the old man's sad face in the small mirror.

I forgot to ask about the freaking mirror.

He turned around, wedging his notes under his arm, hesitated for a bit, and then walked toward the subject, the convicted killer, kidnapper, and rapist Alex Mars, who now lay half-dead and served as a lab rat at The Cooper Institute. Acting on instinct, Daniel half sat on the bed and held Alex's hand. He then looked at the plug of the mechanical ventilator, connected to the wall.

I bet you can't reach the bottom.

He stared at it for a long minute.

"I'm sorry," Daniel said in a trembling voice. He squeezed Alex Mars's hand, bending his head down. Then he let go, stood up, and left the room.

Daniel was about to enter the cafeteria when Dr. Jerry Shoop called him from the other side of the hallway.

"Daniel! I'm glad I found you. How are things going?"

Daniel looked at Dr. Shoop with a fake smile. "Things are going well. Just cleared my desk, so I guess we won't be neighbors anymore."

Dr. Shoop smiled and slapped him lightly on the back. "I've heard you did a great job. Well, listen. I was looking for you because I didn't have a chance to tell you yesterday. Usually on Saturdays all the researchers go out on the town for some food and a drink or two. Considering you just finished your first week here, this could be your welcome party. What do you say?"

"That sounds like a great idea. It'll be a distraction from my thoughts, and it'll be good to get to know everyone better."

"Perfect. Let's meet in the lobby in about thirty minutes."

Daniel found the whole research crew in the lobby. Dr. Cowen was wearing a tucked blue button-down with khakis and neat shoes, and Dr. Shoop wore a simple white T-shirt with "Dewey Beach" written on it, black shorts, and flip-flops. Kelly stood there, her short, black hair groomed to one side, wearing jeans overalls and a long-sleeve cotton shirt with black and white stripes.

"There he is. The cab is waiting for us outside," Dr. Shoop said, and the others turned and greeted him.

Kelly waved, and Dr. Cowen gestured with his head, keeping his hands in his pockets.

"Hello, everyone," Daniel said with enthusiasm. He hoped tonight would help break the ice a bit.

They stepped out and into the cab. Dr. Shoop gave Daniel a card with the taxi's information and checked he brought his ID. Otherwise, it would be a pain to get back inside. Then he told a story about the time he lost his ID when he was still an intern and spent half of the night trying to find it, only to realize that Lucas, a former coworker, had hidden it from him.

"And then as I was basically crying to the bartender, this guy sits on my right and goes, 'You might need this' and slides me my ID."

Dr. Shoop was laughing out loud, and Dr. Cowen was smiling, though it looked like a grimace. Kelly and Daniel both looked at each other and smiled. It was hard not to with someone like Dr. Shoop bursting out laughing like that.

They arrived at a pub called Indigo, which was decently crowded, with a couple of pool tables, darts, and a long wooden bar top, behind which were two bartenders.

"Who wants a drink?" Dr. Shoop asked loudly. "First round is on me!" he said as the group sat at a round table next to a window.

The waitress came, and he ordered Bud Ices for everyone. Daniel could not avoid hearing that creepy penguin commercial in his head:

Doo-be, do-be, do…

"A toast for our new member! Mr. Daniel Spence!" said Dr. Shoop.

"Cheers!" everyone answered, and clinked their bottles.

The music was great, ranging from Bruce Springsteen to Led Zeppelin and more. Daniel liked the vibe, and it seemed like everyone else did too.

"This bar is pretty good," Daniel said to the group, and to his surprise, Dr. Cowen was somewhat friendly in response.

"Well, don't say that to Dr. Cooper. One time we tried to make him come with us. This was like, what, five years ago?" He looked over at Dr. Shoop for confirmation, and he nodded, smiling. "And his response was 'I think I'll pass, but thanks. My days of wild drinking are behind me, and the best bar in town was Skellar, not that Indigo slum you guys go to.'"

Everyone burst out laughing.

Dr. Shoop added, "Hey, the man has being working here for ages. He probably knows this town inside out."

The night went smoothly. They ordered burgers and a second round, and everyone seemed to have a good time, even Dr. Cowen, who was a bit more relaxed. They talked about football and how Dr. Shoop thought the Cowboys would be unstoppable next season.

"I think the Packers have a chance. Brett Favre is a beast," Kelly said as she finished her third beer.

"You Americans and your 'football.' That shit isn't football, that's American football," Dr. Cowen said in his low voice, a bit of an accent slipping in. "The real football is what you guys call soccer. That's the sport everyone else in the world loves."

Everyone looked at him and laughed again.

The conversation moved on, and now everyone told Daniel a little about themselves. He found out that Dr. Cowen was from New York, born and raised by immigrant parents who were escaping World War II. His accent came to the surface after a couple of drinks. Kelly was born and raised in Chicago, went to Illinois Institute of Technology for undergrad, and was in her third year of grad school. Finally, Dr. Shoop told them about his childhood in Dewey Beach, Delaware. He loved surfing and football and went to Penn State University for undergrad and grad school. He told them about the bad injuries he suffered to his leg and ribs after a terrible accident while surfing and, of course, he showed them the large scar that ran from his abdomen down the back of his leg.

"I think I've heard about your surfing injury about thirty-seven thousand times," Dr. Cowen said, crossing his arms, and both Kelly and Daniel laughed.

"Hey, it's a good story. Now stop complaining. You and I have to settle important matters," Dr. Shoop responded.

"What important matters?" Kelly asked in sheer curiosity.

"Ah, Dr. Cowen over here has never been able to beat me at billiards," Dr. Shoop said in a quirky voice.

"Here we go again. Come on, let's get it over with," Dr. Cowen responded in his low voice.

Both men stood up and went towards the other side of the bar to the tune of "Born in the USA." Daniel looked at Kelly, who was watching them, and then he broke the silence. "It amazes me how much Dr. Cowen changes when he is not at the institute."

"You are telling me," Kelly said, still staring at them. "That guy is usually the grumpiest man alive, but give him two beers and he is someone else. It's like Dr. Jekyll and Mr. Hyde, sort of."

Daniel smiled. After all the booze and the good conversation, he finally felt more comfortable—more part of the team, you could say. He looked out the window and saw a tall person standing on the street corner opposite. It seemed to be a woman, judging by her long black hair, but there was something familiar about her…

"Hey, about the other day," Kelly said with a touch of shame.

Daniel looked back at her. "Don't worry about it. I was out of line." Daniel sipped his beer. "Mind if I ask you something?" he asked, and quickly turned his head to look again at that familiar woman, but she was gone.

"I think I know where this is going, but sure."

"In that argument you said, 'What we are working toward in the institute is larger than whatever I could imagine.' What did you meant by that?" Daniel said, lowering his voice, despite the loud music.

Kelly looked around, hesitated a bit, then leaned forward, and whispered, "Listen, Daniel, The Cooper Institute is"—she glanced over her shoulder and looked around—"a dangerous place. In the past six months I've worked there I've seen things."

"What things?" Daniel's senses focused on Kelly.

"At first I thought we were studying dreams. But then I saw the experiments we ran. They changed the subjects. It seems as if everything we do breaks a switch here." She pointed at her forehead.

Daniel thought of his first subject, Alex Mars, and could not help but feel sick to his stomach. The guilt was coming back, and it didn't combine well with the five beers or so he drank. He pushed the thoughts away. "So you think The Cooper Institute is running unethical experiments. But to what end?"

Everything you think you know about the human mind is a lie.

"I don't know. I haven't been able to go that far. But part of you knows that things are not okay here." Kelly's eyes were big and seemed to be begging for something.

"How are you so certain?" Daniel said.

"I saw you earlier today. I wanted to talk about our little disagreement, so I went to your experiment room to see if you were there. But the door was slightly ajar, and I saw you holding the subject's hand. That's when I knew you felt it too. That's when I knew I could trust you."

Daniel remained quiet for a bit, embarrassed at being caught doing that. It was just an impulse, nothing more.

Kelly carried on. "You are only going to be here for a year, I have six months left. I want to—no, I need to—know what is happening here." Looking down at the table, she added, "I need to know that everything I've done was worthwhile."

"What things have you done?"

"That's a conversation for another day. We don't have much time now. So, will you work with me? We can help each other?"

Daniel looked into Kelly's eyes to see if she was lying and saw that she wasn't. He was as eager to know more about this place as she was. But he also knew she was a step behind him, based on what Dr. Cooper told him:

Very few people at the institute know about this. In fact, only Dr. Shoop and Dr. Cowen know too. That's because when they performed this experiment, they found the images, and questioned them. They stopped and took a step back to see what they meant, what all this could really mean.

He never mentioned Kelly. So it would be safe to assume that her path at the institute was probably very different from the one he would experience. Still, she has been at the institute longer and had seen more things. There was nothing to lose through having a second source of information about the place. As for how much information he would share with her, that remained to be seen.

"All right, let's do it," Daniel said, and drank a sip of his now-warm beer. "Why did you say to drop the detective role back in the institute? Was that just an act? Is there any sort of surveillance?"

"Yes, at least that's my assumption. I haven't seen many cameras, but I'm sure the whole place is bugged. If the government is involved, then I don't trust having conversations there. I prefer to be cautious."

"Well, we need a safe place to discuss things if we are going to keep each other informed. What about the rooms? We can check mine for bugs. If there aren't any, that could be a place. I can check for them tonight and, worst comes to the worst, we can revisit next week on our break."

Kelly thought about it for a second, then agreed. She looked over and saw Dr. Cowen and Dr. Shoop approaching the table, so she rushed to say something.

"One last thing, Daniel," she said, her voice barely audible. "From now on, be very careful."

Daniel walked into his room using the wall for balance and turned the light on. He was decently intoxicated and pretty fatigued; his body was finally getting used to the graveyard shift, but combining that with drinking had been a terrible idea. Daniel sat on his bed, still thinking about his conversation with Kelly. He wondered how much Kelly had experienced. Now that he was drunk, he allowed himself to think back to the dream. He let himself go even further, remembering the first nightmare he had here, that presence he felt in the library. Could Kelly be experiencing these intense nightmares? Those white marbles and greenish-white feet—had Kelly seen them too? Even worse, could that be linked to his second dream? Then he had a sharp realization:

You felt the same uncanny emotion when you experienced both of them. But that did not mean much, did it? No, and this was all speculation. Correct? Yes. So, then, there is no point in speculating without enough information, which would just be a waste of time.

With that settled, Daniel stood up and went into his bathroom to take a quick shower. Inside, the warm water dripped down his face, relaxing him. He was still a bit tipsy, but the effects of the alcohol were wearing off thanks to the two glasses of water he drank before coming back from the bar. As the shampoo slid over his closed eyes, for an unknown reason he felt the need—no, an urgency—to open his eyes and check around. Then his rational mind kicked in.

Human imagination is fertile and brilliant. It is at its peak when we are kids, and the rational thoughts that govern our world as adults are no more than guests, ones whom you can choose to ignore out of interest or fear. In fact, I would dare to say that every adult knows that kids are crazy but have a firm belief that their irrationality is just temporary. Yet from time to time, even adults have small moments of fantastic imagination. You don't believe me? Tell me you haven't heard a sound in your basement and felt scared, even though the most dangerous thing you could find is a mouse or a raccoon. Or what about what is happening to me right now? When you are in the shower, at that moment when the shampoo is sliding off your head and down your face, and as you keep your eyes closed, you can't help to feel a bit uncomfortable. For a kid, the world is full of irrational and fascinating thoughts; for an adult, the world is full of rational thoughts, and these "moments of fantastic imagination" that are the norm in our childhood are reduced to minor spikes in particular situations. But that does not make them any less fascinating and, in fact, it increases their worth. You know I'm right because as you open your eyes and check on that shower, you smiled, relieved to find it empty.

Regardless of this irrational impulse, followed by his rational thoughts, Daniel did, in fact, feel something different. He felt a second body there with him. His first impulse was to keep his eyes closed; he was afraid of what he might see. Then the voice of adulthood spoke in his head.

Childish... Open your eyes, Spence.

He opened them slowly. Nothing. He was the only one in the shower. A nervous smile appeared on his face.

He finished, stepped out of the shower, and dried himself. Daniel left the bathroom, completely ignoring the naked white figure with long black hair in the mirror which hung on his closet.

Daniel turned off the room lights and turned on the desk lamp. He grabbed his dream journal to read the poem, as he always did before bed, but something strange happened. He could not read the words. Instead of letters there were scrawls. Confused, he closed the journal. Someone with a pale face and long black hair was just a few inches from him. Grinning at him, staring back with white eyes—white marbles without pupils. Daniel was terrified that

that face was looking at him, inside of him. The pale body attached to the face was on top of his; he felt petrified. He could not move a muscle. He wanted to scream, shake that thing off, run away, run out of that room, run to his car and drive far away. The pale face tilted to the right ever so slightly, its creepy smile getting wider…

He woke up abruptly, covered in sweat and hyperventilating. He lay there, confused, not sure where reality stopped and this dream started. It took a minute for Daniel to calm his thoughts. He sat on the bed again, sweat sliding off his wet hair. Whatever that thing was, he knew in his gut it was the same one he saw at the library. Not sure of what to do next, he grabbed his dream journal, now relieved he could read the poem, and started writing.

CHAPTER 10

AFTER A RESTLESS evening, Daniel woke up exhausted with a slight hangover. He got ready, grabbed a quick dinner of blueberry pancakes and syrup with orange juice, and was at Dr. Cooper's office around 7 p.m.

"Good evening, Dr. Cooper. Are you ready for me?" Daniel asked after he knocked and peeked in.

The old man sat at his desk reading some documents. He had a red pen he was using from time to time to mark things up and make notes. His blue eyes met Daniel's, and a slight smile appeared on his face. "Yes, Mr. Spence, come on in."

Daniel did. Dr. Cooper put the papers away. "How was your first break here in Ashfield?"

"It was quite entertaining. I must say I was pleasantly surprised," Daniel said, and smiled.

"I knew you were going to find the beauty in this small town eventually. It'll only get better, I promise." Dr. Cooper took off his glasses, grabbed a small cloth from his lab pocket, and started to clean them methodically. "Before we go, I wanted to hear your opinion on something."

"Oh sure. What is it?"

"What's your take on dreams?" Dr. Cooper asked as he continued his methodical cleaning.

"Dreams? A dream is a series of thoughts, images, and sensations occurring in a person's mind during sleep," Daniel answered as he reclined back in his chair and crossed his arms.

Where is he going with this?

"Great definition, but I asked for your opinion," Dr. Cooper said, still focusing on the glasses.

"My opinion…" Daniel put his hand under his chin and thought for a moment. A small grin appeared on his lips. "It's funny you ask that. Before I started working here, I would have said that it's just our brains sorting information from our day and deleting information that is not needed. Like hitting the reset button on a computer. But now that we have proven the existence of something that goes beyond the brain, I guess I'm not sure what to think of a lot of things anymore."

Dr. Cooper stopped and gave Daniel a studious look. "That's a better answer. Given what we have discovered here, there are no limits anymore. The possibilities are endless."

"What do you mean?"

"Dreams have been a huge part of humanity. They have helped shape religions, like Judaism, Christianity, Islam, Hinduism, etcetera. They have been part of our lives for thousands of years, and we as a species have gone to great lengths to record these fantastical events. But religion is just the tip of the iceberg. Look at all the art, the philosophy, the literature." Dr. Cooper's voice was both soft and had a tinge of amazement in it, as if he were talking about his biggest passion.

Daniel leaned forward and placed his elbows on the table, keeping his hands together in front of his chin as he spoke. "I see now. Before, we could dismiss those ideas as sheer human curiosity or just interpretations to justify the unknown," he said in a confident tone. "Then you add to the equation the fact that the brain is just producing all of these images, and there is your rational explanation. But we have proven that you can take the brain out of the equation and still have dreams. Therefore, as of now there isn't much of a rational explanation."

"Exactly. So now every possibility is on the table. And you are as open to them as I am. If I just handed you the results of that experiment, then you could have your doubts. But because you came to the same conclusion on your own, we are now on the same page." Dr. Cooper checked his silver pocket watch and looked back at Daniel. "Now that things are clear, I think it's best for me to tell you the hypothesis that we are exploring with this new experiment. Please allow me to finish; then I can answer any questions you may have." He smile briefly, then continued. "Based on past studies, we want to prove that dreams are the manifestation of the mind in a different dimension. When we are awake, our rational mind is in control, and things around us follow a specific logic that our brain can and will process. But in our dreams, there are no laws, or at least no laws our brain can comprehend. No, this dreamland, this dimension, is for the mind, for everyone's mind. I call it the Theory of the Reverie."

After a moment's silence, Daniel finally shared his thoughts. "My initial impulse is to fully reject your theory. There is just nothing that backs it up. It's one thing to say that the mind and brain are separate, and another thing to state that our minds manifest in a different dimension when we sleep. But then again, you aren't giving me all the information, are you? What past studies have you done that back up your theory?"

Dr. Cooper closed his eyes and took a deep breath. His voice came out a bit shaky, and Daniel could clearly saw the old man tightly holding his fingers. "I'm afraid I can't tell you, Mr. Spence."

"Why not?"

Dr. Cooper turned slightly to the left in his chair and looked up toward the wall, and Daniel could see he was lost in thought. "I'm afraid you are not ready yet. None of you are. Both Dr. Cowen and Dr. Shoop have also being eager to know the reasoning behind my theory, the experiments that put me on this path a long time ago when it was just myself and my research. But for all of your sakes, I need you to trust me."

Daniel remained silent and looked at Dr. Cooper's face. The man was old all right, but Daniel always perceived him as strong—not physically but mentally. Yet for the first time since his arrival, he saw weakness.

"What is the point of telling me this theory if you are not going to share any details that would help me believe it? Regardless of what I believe, I'll still go through with the experiment, given my role as an intern. So why go to the trouble of sharing this with a week-old intern?"

His question was followed by a long silence.

"I needed you to know what's at stake, what we are aiming for here. I do not want you to think we are dealing with simple dreams anymore. This could be much more complex and rich than that." Dr. Cooper turned back and looked at Daniel. "You think you can handle it?"

"Yes, I do," Daniel said in a low voice. He realized he was challenging Dr. Cooper, the leading psychologist of the century. He could almost hear the disapproving voice of his father in the back of his mind, and felt ashamed. "I'm sorry, Dr. Cooper. It's not my place to question your theories—after all, I'm just an intern."

"Not at all, Mr. Spence. Your ability to question is one of the reasons you are here. Besides, if the experiment succeeds, a lot more answers will come to both of us. If it fails—well, then, you must indulge this old man the occasional mistake."

Daniel smiled. Dr. Cooper took out his silver pocket watch again and glanced at it.

"We should go. Dr. Cowen is probably waiting for us downstairs by now." He put his watch back and looked at Daniel. "I'm sure I don't need to say this, but just a reminder: this is all confidential, and I'm expecting your discretion, Mr. Spence."

"Of course, Dr. Cooper," Daniel said in a respectful tone.

The elevator doors opened on Level 3, and Dr. Cooper led Daniel through the hallway. They were quiet most of the way, so Daniel speculated about what could possibly be next. Based on all the conversations he had so far, and things he had seen, he simply didn't know what to expect anymore.

Using his key, Dr. Cooper swiped on Room 3C, which had a red light above its door. Inside, Daniel found himself in a room that seemed to be half recording studio and half hospital room, the two different sections separated by a thick glass wall divider. They walked into the recording studio portion, which had a black desk with a strange keyboard that had sliders and buttons up against the glass wall. To its right, there was a screen, which Daniel assumed was the DSD, and to the left, there were headphones with a microphone, connected to a black box on the floor. The whole system seemed very sophisticated, like a NASA computer. Curiously, there was a mirror on the desk like the one for the last experiment.

"Good evening, Dr. Cowen. Is everything checked and set up?" Dr. Cooper asked, and that was when Daniel saw Dr. Cowen squatting to his left. He seemed to be calibrating a machine and taking notes.

"Yes, everything is ready, Dr. Cooper." He rose and turned, exchanged looks with Daniel, and saluted him with a head gesture.

Dr. Cooper reached the desk, too, turned, and started his explanation. "This is your new workstation, Mr. Spence. As you can see, the room is divided into two sides: this side is called the Feeder, where the researchers will be, and that side is called the Receiver. That's where the subjects are."

Daniel saw a medical chair surrounded by what he assumed to be medical equipment on the Receiver side.

"I'm sure you are familiar with the term 'lucid dreaming,'" Dr. Cooper carried on.

"Yes, being conscious during your dreams; therefore, being able to manipulate them. In other words, having self-awareness while dreaming."

Dr. Cooper smiled. "Precisely. What we want to do here

is to influence a person's dreams by directly communicating with them while they are dreaming. We'll provide them with self-awareness and then explore the effect that this has on the subject, and if we can, we will search for proof that this is a parallel dimension."

That was when everything clicked for Daniel. They were doing pretty much the same thing as in the movies, where you see a bunch of people with headphones trying to communicate with an astronaut on the moon, except they were communicating with someone who was dreaming—who was, according to Dr. Cooper's theory, in a different dimension, in a reverie.

"I see. But what type of directions should we give them? Is there anything specific?" Daniel asked.

"Dr. Cowen is familiar with some of the commands, but basically ask them to manipulate their surroundings. Ask them to shape their environment, or do extraordinary things, like flying. This will not come easy or fast. A lot of the time, the subject panics or doesn't know how to handle the situation. Therefore, the more times we can connect with them, the easier it gets to influence them. It'll take you two a bit." Dr. Cooper checked his silver pocket watch. "Well, it looks like I need to get going. Come to me if you make any significant discoveries. Otherwise, we can revisit in two weeks. With the basics we discussed, Dr. Cowen can take it from here."

"Of course, Dr. Cooper," he said in an obedient voice.

"Good. Mr. Spence, if you need anything, Dr. Cowen will be able to assist you. You two will be working together here, although he'll need to step out from time to time. The three of us can meet again in two weeks after you collect some data, unless you can establish a major connection. Any questions?"

"No, sir, I think I got everything," Daniel said.

"All right, then, good luck, you two," Dr. Cooper finished, and walked away.

"Come join me, Mr. Spence," Dr. Cowen said as he sat down in one of the two rolling chairs of the large desk.

Daniel felt strange as he inspected the complex keyboard once he had sat down. There was a set of buttons with labels below them and sliders above each one. Terms like "SLEEP," "ESC," and "REM" stood out from the rest. Dr. Cowen handed a small book to Daniel.

"Here is a manual with a detailed explanation of everything, but in a nutshell, this keyboard controls the different gases that we administer to the subject. The gases are designed at The Cooper Institute to provoke sleep and generate faster and longer REM cycles."

Daniel grabbed the book and put it to the side. Dr. Cowen's tone had changed slightly from the condescending, bored one he had when he gave Daniel the tour of the place. It took Daniel a moment to realize there was a touch of respect in his voice. He was addressing him the same way he would a professional colleague rather than a useless intern.

"There are three buttons and their sliders that matter for this experiment. All of them work on the same principle. When the button is pressed, the sliders unlock. They should all be slid all the way to the left every time a new experiment starts, which means naught percent of the gas is supplied. Clearly, as you slide it, the percentage increases. That's why you have those ten white lines to guide you."

Dr. Cowen drank a bit of his coffee, then proceeded.

"The first button that matters to us is obviously 'On,' which is pretty self-explanatory. The second one is "SLEEP." It administers a similar gas to what anesthesiologists use before surgery to get subjects to fall asleep faster. The third one is 'REM.' Basically, it filters a second gas that will change the sleep cycle of the patient and allow it to go straight to the REM, or rapid-eye-movement, stage, which is important to us because?"

"It's the stage where our brain is active and we dream."

"Exactly. So this gas helps us skip over the cycles of sleep we do not need."

"So, then, if we have this gas, why is it important to run the experiment at night?" Daniel asked, crossing his arms and reclining his wheeled leather chair back a bit.

"Great question. The answer is simple: it will take more time, gas, and money to make someone sleep during the day for the periods of times that we want. I discovered that it was better to administer the gas during the body's normal sleep cycle. Faster results, saves time, saves money." He said this last part with pride. For someone who could be classified as rational and calculating, Dr. Cowen had moments where it was impossible for him to hide his emotions. Especially his pride.

He drank another sip of coffee and continued. "The last button is 'ESC.' If things go... wrong, you click that button, and the system will shut off. The gas will be cut off, and the subject will eventually wake up on their own. You can call the nurses by pressing it three times in a row."

"What do you mean, if something goes wrong?" Daniel asked as he reclined further.

"Something out of the ordinary happens. There are subjects who could still have some body movement."

"You mean somnambulism?"

"That's one example, but it could also be any type of abnormal movement for a sleeping person. I'm sure it'll be fine. I haven't used it yet." He grabbed a pack of cigarettes from his lab coat and placed one in his mouth. He offered one to Daniel.

"Quit a long time ago, but thanks," Daniel said as he waved his hand.

"Fair. I've been trying to quit for a while now. Anyway, shall we begin?" he asked, placing a cigarette between his lips.

"Let's do it." Daniel leaned forward and sat straight, ready for action.

Dr. Cowen pushed the "READY" button, which lit up in a green color. Then he reached in a cabinet. He handed Daniel a booklet and a second headset. "It's better if we have a second pair of ears. That way, you can familiarize yourself with the system as well. But for now, just let me do the talking."

Is this guy really the same one I met a week ago?

Daniel put on the headset but bent the microphone upwards, away from his mouth, following Dr. Cowen's instructions.

"Do you like fishing, Mr. Spence?"

Daniel was thrown off by the question but played along. "Yeah, I used to go with my dad when I was little. Why?"

Dr. Cowen blew out a cloud of gray smoke, then continued with a wide grin on his face. "Because we are going fishing, Mr. Spence, but we'll be in a pond of dreams instead of a lake. And instead of fish, we don't really know what is in this pond…Even better, we don't know what we'll catch."

CHAPTER 11

A DISCREET DOOR opened, and two nurses—a muscular black man, and a ginger-haired man with an excessive amount of freckles—escorted a small woman in. With dark spots below her eyes, blond and messy hair, and a couple of early wrinkles, she seemed tired and sick. She gave the impression of being homeless, even though her white hospital gown was neat and had the insignia "3-56B."

My God, she is a mess. Did we do this?

Despite her appearance, her expression seemed distant and relaxed. The two nurses led her to the hospital bed, where she lay down. They connected her to the medical equipment that would monitor her vital signs throughout the experiment. Daniel saw how the ginger-haired nurse was carefully grooming the subject's hair into a ponytail. Once she was all set up, the other nurse grabbed a set of what seemed to be electrodes from behind the bed and placed them neatly on a small silver table next to it. Then he took one, inserted a type of transparent gel, and passed it to the other nurse, who placed it at a specific place on the subject's head. This strange but hypnotizing process was repeated at least twenty times, and by the end, her whole head was covered with electrodes.

"Hey, Dr. Cowen, are those electrodes used for the DSD?"

Dr. Cowen kept his eyes focused on the subject. "Yes, half of them are at least. You probably noticed that half of them are red and the others are black. The red ones are used for the DSD, and the black ones are used for electroencephalography, or EEG. I'm sure you are familiar with the term."

"Well, yeah, but I notice the subject still has hair. Usually, for an EEG to detect the electrical activity in the brain, the patient needs to have their hair shaved off; otherwise, it'll interfere with the record of the electrical activity of the brain."

"Good observation, but do you see how Jack grabbed each electrode and placed a gel on the end? That's a special gel designed by Dr. Cooper a couple of years ago. He said that before, he could only use men for the experiment, because women were not up for having their heads shaved. Imagine if we still needed to shave them. Half of this town would look like they are part of a cult or something." Dr. Cowen half smiled. "This way is more human."

This last statement surprised Daniel in the best of ways. "Yeah, that makes sense."

The subject lay back on the bed, which was partially angled forward so that both Daniel and Dr. Cowen could see her upper body clearly. The two nurses did a final check, gave a thumbs-up, and walked away.

"Hello, Elizabeth. My name is Dr. Viktor Cowen," Dr. Cowen said in a calm and patient voice. "I'm here with Mr. Daniel Spence, my assistant. We'll be with you throughout the experiment. How are you feeling? If you are ready, give me a thumbs-up."

Elizabeth looked up but seemed to have her eyes fixed somewhere above their heads. She raised her hand and gave the thumbs-up. Dr. Cowen looked at Daniel and assented with his head, then covered the microphone with his hand and said, "The glass wall that separates us is actually a one-way mirror, so she can't see us, only her reflection. Anyways, there is no need to go all the way to a hundred percent, especially given the size, weight, and gender of the subject. Based on her file, she is eighty-two pounds and five foot four inches tall. Check page four of the booklet. You'll see a chart."

Daniel did and found out that she only needed thirty to forty percent. He pressed the on button and heard a similar sound to what someone would hear when they turn a computer on with Windows 95. Then he pressed the "SLEEP" button and slid the slider slowly, leaving it at 30 percent. In a matter of ten seconds, the subject's eyes closed, and just like that she was asleep.

"Now we wait around ten minutes. I'm starting my chronometer now." Dr. Cowen looked at his watch and pressed a button.

As time passed, Daniel thought of Dr. Cooper's wild theory. He speculated based on the already improbable assumption that indeed it was possible for our mind to leave our body and manifest itself in a different dimension. Even if he accepted that as a fact, how would they prove it by doing this? Was there one dimension for each person, or was it a shared space? And even if all of this turned out to be true, what practical use could be gotten out of it? Maybe it could serve as a healing tool, or be used for spying, even though spying on the Soviets was a thing of the past. He was still missing a lot of pieces to this puzzle.

"We got an early start, Mr. Spence."

Daniel looked at the screen and saw an image slowly fading in. The point of view was from the subject's perspective. They could see what she could. It was as if they were inside her head. As the image came into focus, Daniel heard a sound. It sounded far away at first, and there was a bit of static, but it slowly became clearer and louder. It was Elizabeth's breathing. As she looked around, Daniel and Dr. Cowen could see where she was: it looked like an airport terminal, with blue carpeting, white walls, and a high ceiling.

She got up and walked away from the terminal entrance, through a long, white, large space into a street. It seemed to be late at night, but the dark cobbled street was clearly visible, with tones of gray and blue. It had the feel of an old European city, with low buildings to each side. Elizabeth walked with determination as the lights in the houses went on.

"Elizabeth, can you hear me?"

Dr. Cowen's voice came as a whisper in Daniel's headset. Elizabeth kept her pace, without responding. From time to time, she looked at a specific detail of a house, like the round amber glass in one, or the large rusty iron doors of another. She also focused on more unconventional details, like the house with a hundred small windows no larger than five inches tall, and the one with windows and doors that looked like a large face that was smiling uncannily. The little town seemed normal at first, but as time passed, Daniel could see irregularities that gave it an eerie feel.

"Elizabeth, if you can hear me, stop walking, please."

Dr. Cowen's voice was louder and more confident, but what he said had no effect.

That was when Daniel heard it for the first time. It slowly faded in, but it was a sound that seemed to have always been there. Bells—church bells to be exact.

"Oh, I'm going to be late!" Elizabeth said as she rushed downhill, running in the middle of the street.

She looked up, and Daniel could see what looked like a small chapel at the end.

"Elizabeth, you are not late. You are just dreaming. You are in the middle of an experiment. Please tell me what time it is." Dr. Cowen sounded impatient.

She reached the small chapel, which was surrounded by people. Or at least that was what Daniel assumed. They looked like shadows in the poor light. Elizabeth excused her way inside. The volume of the bells increased as she stood in what seemed to be a beautiful space with high ceilings, details of gold and marble on the walls, and rows of occupied tables all the way to infinity. In contrast with outside, this place was full of natural light, with windows that went from floor to ceiling on each side. It was like a college library in finals week.

Dr. Cowen took a deep breath. "Elizabeth, I need you to focus. Tell me what time it is."

As she rushed through the rows of tables, Daniel could appreciate the level of detail in each person. Some were girls, others were guys, and all of them wore white shirts. Some held a pencil, others were resting their head in their hands, their arms on the table, while yet others were looking up. The only thing they had in common was that none of them looked back at Elizabeth. She, on the other hand, didn't seem to care. She seemed to be focused on finding a spot somewhere to sit. The scene felt more bizarre as Daniel heard Elizabeth's steps bouncing in the space in parallel with the increasing sound of the bells.

"Elizabeth, please focus. What time it is? Isn't it strange that outside was dark and in here is sunny? Isn't that strange?" Dr. Cowen waited, but the scene carried on, with Elizabeth now rushing through the interminable rows, trying to find a seat. He turned the microphone up, rubbed his face with both hands, and took a deep breath.

Following nothing but his gut, Daniel lowered the microphone of his headset and spoke softly. "Hello, Elizabeth, my name is Daniel Spence. If you can hear me, please slow down. We are trying to help you."

Suddenly, Elizabeth stopped. She turned toward one of the windows on her left. The bell sounds were loud and clear now. Daniel saw the perplexed look in Dr. Cowen's face. He looked at the screen and gestured to him to continue.

"Can you hear me?" Daniel asked.

Something changed. It took a minute for Daniel to notice that as Elizabeth slowly approached the window, some of the people sitting down turned and stared at her. A cold, invisible hand touched the back of Daniel's neck and slid down his back with two fingers as he noticed none of them had faces. They lacked eyes, noses, and mouths, but Daniel could still feel how they looked at her. No, not just at her; he could feel how they looked at him too.

She reached the tall window, touched the glass, and slid her hand down.

Suddenly, the bells stopped. The thick sound of silence took over.

"Excuse me. May I help you?" a sweet soft voice came from behind.

Elizabeth turned and saw a priest with a sugary smile. The man was probably in his forties, with a bald scalp, and he gave the impression of being a patient old soul.

"No thanks, Father, I'm just looking for a seat," she responded.

All the "people" who were seated turned toward them.

"The Lord will provide," he said, opening his arms and looking up.

She turned back and kept staring at the window. Everything outside of it seemed blurry.

Daniel tried again. "Elizabeth?"

She stood there in silence for a while, just sliding her index finger along the glass. As quickly as they had stopped ringing, the bells started again, this time louder than ever, to the point where Daniel had to take off his headset. The image slowly dimmed, and the dream was over.

Both of them remained silent for a minute or two. Dr. Cowen lighted up another cigarette, using the burning tip of the old one, while Daniel meditated on what he just witnessed.

"That was one of the most bizarre things I've seen," he stated.

"You tell me. I've been working on this kind of experiments for months now, and dreams are as weird as you would expect." He took a drag and blew the smoke upwards. "What's interesting is the change in tone of the dream from the moment you started talking."

They exchanged looks. "I did notice she stopped just when I said something, but the dream carried on. It could very well be a coincidence."

"Indeed. The only way to know for certain is to keep experimenting. But the reactions of her environment and those faceless people are promising. I think we are on the right track." Dr. Cowen looked over at the subject. "Based on her brain activity, she entered the deep-sleep cycle. We'll wait until she is done and then start again."

CHAPTER 12

DESPITE DR. COWEN'S prediction, they did not find anything any more meaningful later. Elizabeth had two more dreams, and they were short. In one, she was on the beach and seemed to be in the body of a little girl. It was sunny, and she spent her time playing in the sand. The one remarkable moment came when she looked at the ocean and saw a giant rock on the horizon. It was foggy on top of it, and it seemed as if the rock was approaching her. The bells rang again, but this time the sound was almost a whisper. Both Daniel and Dr. Cowen tried to contact her, but it was no good. She woke up shortly after.

In the second dream, she was in a small and simple room. She experienced confusion and anxiety because there were voices. They started as whispers and slowly became louder, but she could still not understand what they said. It was as if they were speaking in a different language, one almost diabolic. Both Daniel and Dr. Cowen tried to talk to her, without success, and the dream became more of a torture than anything else. She eventually put herself in a fetal position and started sucking her thumb. Daniel could see how, as she became smaller, the room became larger. The dream eventually ended with the ringing of bells again.

After further discussion, they came to the conclusion that the bells were probably a major recurring feature, and that they would probably encounter them in the future. So next time they would focus their directions on the bells, and maybe that would be the key to her awareness and make her lucid. With that plan in place, Dr. Cowen called it a night and finished the first session of the experiment.

Daniel was both exhausted and starving, so he stopped at the cafeteria for a quick bite. It was only 5 a.m., a couple of hours before regular breakfast, so the place was deserted. He grabbed some yogurt and fruit and sat at a table toward the middle. Every step he took resonated in the space and was amplified by its emptiness, but Daniel did not notice. He was submerged in a sea of thought.

Providing awareness to people's minds in their dreams. Using them as explorers and guinea pigs of this shared dimension. Could we even say it's a shared dimension, or does each person have their own? And that's assuming the whole dimension part is true. Then again, we proved that the mind and brain are separate—no question about that. But we also proved that the brain is needed to create any sort of real three-dimensional imagery like that which Elizabeth showed today, compared to the broken sentence Alex Mars had "spelled" to him during the last experiment. Broken brain, broken dimension? This is just too far out there, and yet part of me...

The sound of a piece of silverware hitting the floor brought him back with a jump. He looked around and realized he was alone, so he decided to go to bed, because he was feeling tired (*uneasy*). He cleaned up and took a banana with him. When he got to his room, he tossed the peel away and took a quick shower. It was 5:45 a.m. when he turned off the lights and tried to get some sleep.

Not thirty minutes later a knock on his door woke him up. He rolled to the other side of his bed and tried to ignore it, but the asshole was persistent.

"I'm sleeping," Daniel growled.

"I don't care," Kelly said, and Daniel jumped out.

Shit, with all this, I completely forgot about Kelly.

His drowsy hand moved toward the door handle and unlocked it. Kelly walked in, spilling white light from the hallway all over the room. He blinked multiple times, trying to regain his vision, but that became pointless, because Kelly immediately turned on his room light and made Daniel go blind.

Daniel sat on his bed, his eyes still hurting, as Kelly gave him a piece of paper and looked at him with a finger to her lips. It said, *Did you search for bugs?* Daniel looked at her and made a negative gesture, feeling a little ashamed. She gave a frustrated snarl and proceeded to search his whole room. Daniel got up and did the same, even though he was not exactly sure what bugs looked like. For the next ten minutes, they searched every corner, every inch of the closet, and every light bulb in both the room and the restroom.

"Okay, I believe we are safe," Kelly concluded, and sat on the chair next to the desk and took a deep breath.

"I'm sorry I didn't check for bugs before. So much has happened in the past night, it feels like I haven't talked to you in a month," Daniel said as he walked out of the restroom and sat on the bed.

"Don't worry, I know. This place does that to you.

Sometimes two weeks go by and you won't even realize, and sometimes one night can seem like an eternity." She rubbed her face, then slid her hands to the back of her neck and massaged it. "So, as I told you at the bar, I believe we are running unethical experiments to search for something in dreams. I want to know what your take is on that and what you have learned so far."

The question was a key to open Pandora's box. Back at the bar, Daniel thought of this as highly unlikely. Now, it was a different story. Now, to some degree he knew the crazy theory Dr. Cooper was pursuing. Based on what was done to Alex, one could conclude that ethics at the institute were at best a gray area. But before considering all of this, a more important and pressing question popped into Daniel's mind: *Can I trust her?*

"Hold on a second. You said you've done some things, but you avoided the explanation at the bar. I want to know about that."

Kelly looked at him, then sighed. "All right, I guess I have to earn your trust first. When I started working here, I got assigned the same experiment you did. I showed Dr. Cooper the random images that I got, and he seemed very pleased with my progress. Afterwards I was reassigned to work in the lab, and that's when things started to get ugly. I worked alongside Dr. Cowen for the next couple of months. Our objective was to improve the sleep gas and make sure we were getting as much REM-stage sleep out of the subjects as possible. Do you know how the sleep cycle works?"

Daniel thought for a bit, trying to remember his classes at college. "From what I remember, there are five stages in the sleep cycle, stage one being the beginning, stage four being very deep sleep, and stage five is the REM stage."

"Exactly. On average it can take ninety minutes for a person to enter REM. And in a full night of sleep, the person can have five to six REM stages. Of course, this is very dependent on age and specific individual characteristics. We evaluated three subjects: we got their sleep cycles based on the wavelength their cortical activity produced, which we measured with an EEG. We did this for a month, using the normal sleep gas as our base point."

She paused briefly and changed her position in her chair. Daniel listened carefully from the foot of the bed.

"One of the biggest roles I have had since I got here was in the lab, helping Dr. Cowen developed the different sleep gases. I'm not going to get into the technical details, but we basically added different chemicals to the existing gas, then tested them on mice and other animals. It was a trial-and-error type of experiment." She paused and took a deep breath. "After a lot of attempts, we came up with three different possibilities that were both safe for the subjects and could be potential solutions. This took us around two months, so I was eager to test it out. I was so eager, I was selfish and didn't think what my actions could cause…"

"Bring the last one in," Dr. Cowen said into the microphone on his right as he rubbed his forehead. "All this work, all the different tests we ran, and we find nothing. It seems as if we manage to reduce time in the first and second stages, but then it gets added to the third and fourth. If the last test gas does not work, it'll be a huge failure."

"It'll work, I'm sure of it," Kelly said.

Dr. Cowen looked at her and saw the large black bags beneath her eyes.

"It better, or else…"

"I know, but the G-37 was our best test gas. If that does not work, then we know for certain that the sleep cycles cannot be altered, so it won't be for nothing."

But Kelly was in fact quite sure this would work. After all, she was the one who came up with the chemical composition. For her, the other two test gasses were just Dr. Cowen trying not to have a woman outsmart him.

The last subject walked through the door, escorted by two nurses—a short, brown-haired man with a large back and a big nose, and a black, corpulent man with very short hair and a strong jaw. While the nurses connected him to all the medical equipment, Dr. Cowen lit up a cigarette and leaned back in his chair. Kelly gave the cigarette pack a tempted look, then looked back up at the thick glass and focused on the subject. Most of his scalp was covered with black and red electrodes. The beeping from the EKG that monitored his heart started, and the two nurses gave them a thumbs-up.

"All right, proceed to administer the G-37 gas please. Let's start with forty percent," Dr. Cowen said into a microphone connected to a speaker in the subject's room.

The short nurse grabbed a gas mask that was connected to a green tank next to the bed; it had yellow letters that spelled *"G-37."* He put the gas mask on the subjects and twisted the red valve on the tank to release the gas. Then he seemed to be speaking to the subject, who in less than ten seconds closed his eyes and drifted off to sleep. Dr. Cowen started a chronometer, and the waiting game began.

"First stage achieved. The subject is entering the second stage now, two minutes thirteen seconds," Dr. Cowen said

while looking at both his chronometer and the EEG next to the DSD. Kelly wrote down these values in her notes.

"We are passing the second stage now. The overall time is six minutes fifty-three seconds. What's our status?"

Kelly wrote these values down with a smirk on her face. Compared to the average for this subject, they were thirteen minutes and twelve seconds ahead of schedule, the best results yet. "We are positive thirteen minutes and twelve seconds."

Dr. Cowen glanced at Kelly's note to corroborate her assessment. "The third and fourth phases usually take thirty-three minutes. Here is the real challenge."

Kelly rolled her eyes, while Dr. Cowen wrote down some notes. For the next couple of minutes, silence governed the room. Cold sweat ran down Dr. Cowen's forehead as he finished his cigarette. Kelly could feel her palpitations, and her excitement was transforming into stress.

After minutes that felt like hours, Dr. Cowen spoke. "We are past the third stage."

"We are positive seventeen minutes and five seconds."

The EEG showed large waves now, and the tension increased with every second. These results would define the last three months of research.

Finally, the EEG waves started to flatten out. The DSD next to them turned on as Dr. Cowen looked at Kelly.

"We are twenty-two minutes two seconds positive," she said with a wide smile.

Dr. Cowen smiled a sort of crooked smile and leaned back in his chair, sliding his hands back from his forehead, grooming his hair. "These results are amazing. We'll have to do more testing, but this is quite promising."

"What now?" Kelly asked as she rubbed her forehead. She just realized she had a headache, but the tension earlier had distracted her from the pain.

"Now we wait. We let the subject dream and test how long he dreams for. We'll look for any deviation from our prior data, and if there is one, we'll try to find out if it correlates to the sleep gas or not." He slid backward in his chair and stretched. "I'm gonna get coffee while the dream progresses. Would you mind keeping an eye on it?"

"No!" a high-pitch scream responded. But it was not Kelly. It sounded like it came from far away, and even at low volume, it managed to freeze the back of Kelly's neck.

"No, please don't!" After a couple of seconds of hesitation, they realized where the sound came from: the headphones connected to the DSD, which were placed next to the screen.

"Dr. Co— " Kelly said, but he raised his hand in a gesture that begged silence. He approached the headphones quickly and put them on, lowering the microphone toward his mouth.

"Is everything all right?" He grabbed the manila folder in front of him and skimmed through it quickly. "Kevin? Are you there?"

No response. Even though the EEG showed signs of REM sleep, the DSD was pitch-black.

"Kevin?" The response wasn't a voice but the beeping of the heart monitor, which had jumped to 169 beats per minute.

"Oh shit," Dr. Cowen said as he pressed the "ESC" button and an alarm went off.

Kelly was petrified as the subject started to have violent spasms and his whole body tensed. Foam formed at his mouth and dripped off into the gas mask as his head started twitching.

"*The subject is entering a state of shock. Where are the damn nurses?!*" *Dr. Cowen said, frustrated. Not two seconds later, two nurses came back in and tried to stabilize him. Seconds later, they rolled the subject out of the room as his convulsions continued, his veins now popping out of his skin, his face purple. It seemed as if his head would explode at any second.*

Kelly couldn't stop herself, despite Dr. Cowen screaming for her. Her brain was no longer in charge but her instincts as a human being. She ran to the door and opened it just in time to see the two nurses rolling the subject through the hallway as fast as they could. Those four seconds felt like four hours, in which Kelly could see every detail of the horrific scene. The subject's eyes were looking up into his eye sockets and looked as white as two poached eggs. His convulsions stopped, and the seemingly unconscious man raised his head slightly and looked at her. No, there were no pupils, but he was still looking at her, she just knew it. His face was puffed up and purple with deep-blue veins, but he kept his vision as the nurses dragged him away. And at the last second, he grinned at her.

By the time Kelly finished, her voice was low and shaky, her gaze fixed on the other side of the room. Bemused, Daniel shifted slowly from looking at Kelly's face, his brain working overtime. Did this mean that his recurring nightmare was real? Did it stalk Kelly too? Or was it all a coincidence? It could very well be, but the similarities between the dream he had with Alex and what Kelly experienced were astonishing.

Daniel looked back up and saw a tear sliding down Kelly's face. He snapped back from his thoughts, and without really knowing what to do, he stood up, kneeled next to her chair, and hugged her. "Hey, it wasn't your fault."

Kelly welcomed the hug, and they both sat there quietly for a bit. She pulled back and they exchanged looks.

"Excuse me," she said, and went to the bathroom.

Daniel sat back on the bed. He heard the water running in the sink and felt a node form in his throat. He knew it was time to tell her his experiences, but there was something about the idea of saying it out loud that terrified Daniel. He would be accepting that thing existed, accepting that The Cooper Institute seemed to have no ethics, accepting that Dr. Cooper was convinced of his theory—and was willing to go above and beyond for it, no matter the cost.

She walked back and sat on the chair again. Her look seemed composed; her determination was back.

"So, what happened to you? It's only been a week, but judging by your pale expression, you've seen stuff too."

Daniel looked at her, took a deep breath, and told her what happened with his first subject, Alex. When he finished, Kelly's face was pale.

"This only confirms that whatever I saw is most likely be related to whatever you saw. But what does not seem to fit together is that one event happened while you were asleep, while the other happened when I was awake. At first, I thought that maybe the gas we are using affects an area in their brain and makes them go mad. But you did not use that gas, yet you still saw that reaction. This is all just very confusing."

"It is. I also have a new subject, Elizabeth, and she did not react to the gas like that. So, maybe the gas affects some but not others."

"Maybe." She crossed her arms, appearing slightly frustrated. "But that does not explain your dream. Although I'm sure it is not a coincidence that you dreamed that, and then you woke up and got results."

"Did you ever experience a dream like mine?" Daniel asked.

"Not really, not that I can remember at least," Kelly responded.

"It's like we are missing parts of a puzzle." Daniel thought back to his last meeting with Dr. Cooper and the conversation about his theory, the Reverie. He knew Kelly had no idea about it, but why? She had been here for around six months; he had been here a week. Why hadn't she heard anything? No matter. Kelly had trusted him, and he should do the same.

I think you should not be judging the man who's giving you a job, Daniel, his father's voice came from the back of his head. He tried to ignore him. This was beyond what his stubborn, asshole father would understand. And this theory would send this discussion in the right direction. But something was stopping him. Something was holding him back, but what? Was it Dr. Cooper's personal request to keep it confidential?

Considering the mistakes you have made, I'm surprised you still get job offers. So, don't screw this up, and don't bite the hand that feeds you.

I bet you can't reach the bottom.

The voice came back, this time stronger and accompanied by ghosts from his past.

"Daniel?" Kelly's voice brought him back.

He looked at her. "I'm sorry, this has been a lot to

cope with. Why don't we sleep on everything we discussed so far and revisit this in a couple of days?" His voice was trembling.

"All right. Let's keep each other informed if anything happens. Otherwise, let's just meet sometime in the next couple of days."

Daniel was still lost in thought. "Sure, sounds like a plan." He smiled at her. "Good night, Kelly. Thank you for sharing."

"Likewise," she responded with a smile that sank like a stone in Daniel's stomach. She stood up, placed her hand on his shoulder for a second, and walked out, leaving Daniel with all his thoughts and ghosts to deprive him of sleep.

CHAPTER 13

"THE LORD WILL provide."

The priest's voice was loud and clear through the head-phones. Daniel rubbed his forehead.

"Okay, Elizabeth, look at the man. He has been here before and so have you, because this is a dream."

"Calm down," Dr. Cowen said as he covered his microphone and looked at Daniel. "If we manage to break through now, giving her that much information could start a panic, and she might wake up."

"Sorry…It's just that we've been working with her for almost two weeks now, and nothing has happened," Daniel said.

"I already told you this is like fishing. We need to be patient." Dr. Cowen turned back. "Elizabeth, I need you to breathe in and out slowly."

But Elizabeth was too busy walking through a crowded market, with a lot of eccentric fish Daniel had never seen before. Some of them were brightly colored, and some were still moving and even danced. But after having seen so many of her dreams, Daniel was unimpressed. His routine had become monotonous, and although the dreams varied in content, there were consistencies. The most prominent one was the ringing bells, which were always present and only varied in intensity. Another consistency were the faceless people, to the point where Daniel had gotten used to them. Finally, on occasion the priest would show up and say the same exact line.

The image on the DSD faded out and another dream was over. Dr. Cowen took off his headphones and looked at Daniel. "I know this is frustrating, but we'll get there, I know it."

Even though the words of comfort were welcome and Dr. Cowen had shown unbelievable patience, there was still something bugging Daniel.

He took off his headphones and turned to his supervisor. "Mind if I ask you something personal, Dr. Cowen?"

"Of course."

"When I first met you, I felt like I was always wasting your time. You seemed to almost hate me. Since last weekend, when we went to the bar, and throughout this experiment, you've been a great mentor. What changed?" Daniel looked at him, analyzing every detail of Dr. Cowen's expression.

"You can thank Dr. Cooper for that. After your first experiment, he told us just how quickly you had figured out the whole thing. A week? I spent six weeks, and I was a full-time employee then. After I heard that and saw how impressed he was, I was convinced you were worthy of our time. After all, it's not easy to impress Dr. Cooper."

Daniel looked away, a bit ashamed. If they only knew how he figured it out, how he fell asleep during work, how a bizarre dream was the key.

"Wow…Ah, that's…unexpected," he finally said, trying to cover his shame with humility.

"Well, don't let it get to your head. Just keep up the good work so that we can give Dr. Cooper some good news."

To Daniel, when Dr. Cowen talked about Dr. Cooper, he almost sounded like he was talking about a celebrity. He could sense his admiration in his voice.

"Why do you trust Dr. Cooper so much? I mean, the man is a legend, I know. But you almost seem to—"

"To admire him?" Dr. Cowen said, exchanging a look with Daniel, who nodded.

He looked down toward the table. "Yes, that's a fair assessment. I will tell you if it stays between us. Fair?"

Daniel nodded, and Dr. Cowen carried on. "I'm not a people person. I don't really care for working with, or relating to, people in general. That's one of the reasons I work in this exclusive place in the middle of nowhere. Maybe it's because of my childhood—being an only child, the son of two Holocaust survivors and all that. We didn't have a lot of money either." He drank some coffee and was silent for a while.

"I'm sorry to hear that."

"Oh, doesn't matter. I'm just giving you a bit of context. It usually helps to see the whole picture…Anyway, not a lot of kids wanted to be friends with the poor, quiet Jew from the Holocaust family. It was as if we were taboo, a reminder of the worst things humanity could do. But not everything was bad. I read a lot and got really into science, and my parents' dark past sparked my fascination with human behavior. That gave me really good grades and earned me a scholarship that got me through college with a degree in psychology. But I wanted more. There was still so much to be learned. That's where Dr. Cooper came into play. I've followed the man and his books since high school, and I admire him. College gave me the opportunity to finally meet him after a conference, and we connected so well, we ended up having dinner that night." He smiled, probably remembering some funny moments, or maybe just out of nostalgia. He carried on, still smiling. "I was a senior in college when we had that dinner, and it changed my life forever. We kept in touch, and he eventually offered me a full scholarship for grad school. In return, I would work with him in the summers, and once I was finished, I'd join him for two years in this job. That was nine years ago."

Daniel felt a bit strange. It was as if Dr. Cowen saw Dr. Cooper as a father figure.

"Well, there you have it. Now, since today is Sunday, I need to report to Dr. Cooper. Do you think you can handle the DSD alone?" Dr. Cowen asked as he stood up.

"I got it," Daniel said, and waved at his manager.

"All right," Dr. Cowen concluded as he grabbed his paperwork and notes from the table and walked out the door.

He truly is a strange man.

Daniel check the EEG readings to confirm that it was okay to start a second dream, but he still needed to wait a couple more minutes. As he sat there by himself, the sound of silence became louder, and memories crawled back in.

His moment with Kelly earlier that week puzzled him. He saw her vulnerable side, and he comforted her. Right after that, he had (*lied*) being partially honest to her. He felt guilty of course, and, to an extent, silly because probably nothing would have happened if he told her everything. It was only a rule, a condition for Dr. Cooper's trust. Yet rules were rules, and they were there for a reason.

We told you to stay away from the lake without supervision!

Daniel shivered and pushed the voice away. He checked the EEG readings and was disappointed to see that Elizabeth needed at least another ten minutes. He put his elbows on the table and hid his face in his hands, taking a deep breath. Guilt was the main emotion he felt right now, followed by confusion. As he meditated, an image faded in onto the DSD again. It took Daniel a bit of time to hear the steps coming from the headphones next to him. He looked up and saw Elizabeth walking through a dark alley, so he quickly put on the headphones and adjusted the microphone.

She walked along, looking behind her from time to time. Her breathing was getting heavier. Daniel was intrigued. During all the tests they ran throughout the week, a spontaneous dream never happened without using the gas, so he was somewhat hopeful.

She finally reached the end of the alley and saw a small wooden pier. It was a gloomy day now, and the water seemed more black than blue. She walked toward a small wooden boat and jumped in it with determination. It almost seemed like she had done this before as she untied the knot, and the boat slowly moved away from the pier. She sat there for a second just breathing again, feeling more calm. Daniel could hear the breeze in his headphones and could see the movement of the boat against the small waves. The day was still gray. Elizabeth checked her surroundings and realized she was in the middle of the ocean, with a strange, thin fog around her.

"Elizabeth, can you hear me?" Daniel asked softly, but Elizabeth didn't seem to notice.

She checked her surroundings again, and then she focused on the front of the boat. A greenish old cloth was covering something. With trembling hands, she move part of it, and Daniel could see a small wooden chest sitting there. Elizabeth tried to open it, but it was locked. She tried to force it open but couldn't. Even though it had no lock in it, the chest would not give. She tried again and again and periodically checked her surroundings to make sure no one saw her. It was as if she was hiding something she was ashamed of in that chest.

She was starting to get frustrated when an idea popped into Daniel's head. "You know, Elizabeth, I could help you open that chest."

She stopped and looked around frantically. "Who's there?!" she yelled.

Daniel's eyes opened wide, and he tried to mask the excitement in his voice. "My name is Daniel Spence, Elizabeth. You are a volunteer in our experiment here at The Cooper Institute, remember?"

The bells started ringing again. They were far away, but Elizabeth could still hear them.

"Where are you?" she asked with defiance in her voice.

"I'm at The Cooper Institute, and so are you. You are asleep, Elizabeth. This is all a dream."

Daniel's tone was patient and kind, his heart pounding.

"No, no, no, you are messing with me, aren't you? You want it for yourself! Show yourself now!" She had stood up and was yelling again. The image started to get blurry, and

Daniel knew he was losing her. He had to do something quick, or else she would wake up on her own.

"Now, I don't need whatever is in that chest, Elizabeth. I'm here to help you get it."

The church bells were now louder, as if they were slowly approaching them.

"No, you are not! You just want it for yourself!" she yelled defensively. "Everyone just wants it for themselves!"

"Let's make a deal. To prove that I'm right, I'm going to give you specific instructions in how to open that chest. If it works, you get to enjoy what's inside. If not, I'll leave you alone."

Daniel was improvising now. He didn't actually know how to open that chest, but he needed to keep her attention. The objective here was to instruct the subject in their dreams, and after so many failed attempts, he was determined to keep this going as long as possible, no matter the cost.

"I need you to sit down and take a deep breath."

Elizabeth hesitated but then did as she was told. "That's it. Calm yourself. We'll open the chest together, don't you worry."

"If you are lying, you'll be sorry."

Daniel chuckled. "Don't worry, we got this. Just breathe in and out."

It would have been peaceful if it wasn't for the bells that were now ringing loudly.

"Okay, Elizabeth, I want you to focus your energy on the chest and think about the lock. Imagine how the lock open."

This came from Dr. Cowen's explanation earlier that

week. Whether in between Elizabeth's dreams or during one which was particularly unexciting, Dr. Cowen would take the opportunity to teach Daniel some of the best lucid dreaming techniques. The best way to show the subjects they were dreaming was by anchoring them to their lucidity. *Once the subject becomes aware, they need to stay focused and they need to believe that they are dreaming; otherwise, the lucidity can slip away. We achieve this through stabilization techniques.*

Meditation to relax the mind was the technique Daniel tried to suggest to Elizabeth.

"Feel it and now push it open, Elizabeth. With your mind, push it open."

A loud click came from the chest. She sat there, astonished, not believing what just happened.

"See, I told you this is just a dream."

But Elizabeth was not listening anymore. She opened the chest in a rush. In it, there was another greenish cloth.

"Elizabeth, are you there? Can you hear me?"

No response.

She slowly removed the cloth, and what she found made Daniel's stomach twist. A baby—a dead baby with swollen, greenish skin. It looked like someone had drowned the poor thing and left the body floating for weeks. His eyes where puffed up, so they looked like two indentations in his face. Green liquid was dripping out of his nose and his slightly open mouth. The rest of his body followed a similar pattern. But Elizabeth completely ignored him and reached for something next to him that Daniel hadn't noticed before: a syringe containing a brown substance. She slowly injected herself. A speechless Daniel observed the horrific scene as the bells stopped ringing.

An eerie silence governed the scene for the next couple of seconds. Elizabeth's respiration was slow and heavy as she put her arm around the coffer. The syringe was dangling from her arm in a cringeworthy way. Daniel felt sick and lightheaded, but the dream was far from over. The needle slipped out, and blood dripped from the small puncture. Elizabeth started laughing slowly, her voice childish and relaxed. She watched her blood dripping as she giggled. That was when Daniel snapped back to reality.

"Elizabeth, are you still with me?"

Then the small puncture wound from the needle enlargened. No more blood dripped out, but the small wound stretched sideways. Elizabeth's giggle stopped as she observed the strange line, which was now three inches wide.

A cold electric feeling hit Daniel in the back of his head as the line opened, revealing an eye. With its brown iris and dark pupil dilated to the maximum, it looked straight back at Elizabeth. She screamed as the ringing returned, and she smashed it with her hand. Not two seconds later, a second eye appeared higher in her arm. She yelled again and tried to smack that one, too, but the first one was still there, and a third and a fourth appeared, all in different parts of her arm. She started smacking her arm fanatically and then saw how her other arm now had an eye, then a second one. Soon she was covered in them, all looking at her. She started crying and rolling on the floor of the boat.

"I'm sorry! Please make them stop!"

A desperate Daniel wanted to do something, but his

head was still frozen. It wasn't until Elizabeth screamed the third or fourth plea that he reacted.

"I'm sorry, I'm so sorry. They hurt! Please!" she screamed.

He quickly pressed the "ESC" button, but it had no effect. Then he remembered that the system was off. This was a natural dream, and no REM gas was used; therefore, there was no gas to be cut off.

"Elizabeth, jump off the boat quickly! The cold water will help you!" Daniel yelled.

She dragged herself to the side of the boat, and the whole thing tipped. She fell face-first in the water, and everything went black.

Daniel was breathing heavily, holding his head in both hands. He felt as if he had just killed someone by accident. A heavy regret weighed him down. He was short of breath and felt light-headed. He had no clue that the nightmare was just beginning.

CHAPTER 14

AFTER A SMALL break and a glass of water, Daniel felt better. As disturbing as it had been, it was just a nightmare. They were common and bizarre, so even though it was impactful, he could rationalize it fairly quickly and calm down a little. Still, a small part of him felt responsible, but he pushed the feeling aside.

Twenty minutes later, Elizabeth was ready for another round, based on her EEG readings, but Dr. Cowen was nowhere to be seen. Daniel rolled his chair toward the desk, checked on the medical readings, took a deep breath, and started the gas flow.

A couple of minutes later, an image faded in on the DSD.

Daniel put on the headset and spoke slowly and clearly. "Elizabeth, can you hear me?"

She sat in a crowded place, observing people walking by. It seemed to be an airport, with a dark carpet and blue columns and a typical gypsum ceiling. She was constantly rubbing her face and looking around. Daniel's voice made her stop and fix her gaze on the floor.

"Who are you?"

Elizabeth's voice sounded distant and tired, but Daniel was glad she was not freaking out.

"My name is Daniel Spence, Elizabeth. You are in the middle of an experiment."

"An experiment?"

"Yes, you are currently at The Cooper Institute, sleeping, remember?"

"The...Cooper Institute...I see. Yes, that's true I... remember. Who are you?" Her voice came in a light, high-pitched tone, and that was when Daniel realized it was the voice of a child.

"I'm Daniel Spence, the leading...doctor in the experiment tonight. How are you feeling?"

"Okay, cool. I'm good, I think. This feels weird."

A childish giggle came through the headset, and Daniel smiled.

"I know, I agree it is weird, but don't worry. It will be over soon."

"Okay."

"Could you please stand up and stretch your hands forward?"

Elizabeth did, and Daniel saw two small hands extending forward.

"Very good! Now I need you to walk forward."

"Where do you want me to go?"

"Just go forward and we'll find a door or an entrance we can use."

Elizabeth walked for a couple of minutes. She went down a long hallway with hardwood floors and random doors on each side. Bells started faintly ringing in the background.

"Daniel?"

"I'm still here, Elizabeth."

"I'm scared." Her voice trembled, and Daniel could not avoid feeling guilty.

"Don't worry, everything is under control. Why don't we try to walk down to one of the doors?"

"Okay." She stopped in front of a red door. "Does this one seem okay?"

"That one is perfect, Elizabeth."

She opened the door and went in. She was in a small wooden church now, walking in the middle aisle between two rows of pews. It was well illuminated by a long skylight that followed the main aisle. The altar was simple, with a red carpet and a wooden cross. The colored-glass windows behind it gave it a mystical appearances, as multiple colors filtered through and illuminated the space. The bells were louder now. The church was full of people, who were sitting down, facing the altar.

"All right, Elizabeth, you are doing amazing. Now walk toward the altar," Daniel said.

He knew they would find the priest soon. He was almost as ubiquitous as the bells.

She took the first step, and suddenly the bells stopped ringing. Daniel's senses sharpened, and he focused on the DSD. As she slowly walked down the main aisle, the faceless heads of the people turned around slowly.

"I'm scared," she said as she stopped halfway along. The faceless people gave the space an eerie feel, but Daniel had seen them before and knew they were harmless. Now that he had a strong connection with Elizabeth and she was following his instructions, he wanted to explore and give her as many commands as possible.

"Don't worry, Elizabeth, I'm here with you. I promise nothing will happen. Do you recognize this place?"

"Yes…It's familiar, but I can't remember from where."

She kept walking slowly, the sound of her steps resonating in the space. Elizabeth stopped before the altar and started hyperventilating. Daniel saw that her heart rate was increasing, and the image was getting blurry.

"I need you to calm down, Elizabeth. You are in a dream, and nothing can hurt you here," Daniel said patiently.

"That's not true!" she protested as panic took over, and she started to shiver. Elizabeth hugged herself and looked around, moving frenetically. "He did it once, he can do it again. He did it one, he can do it again. He did it once, he can do it again."

She fell to her knees and started crying. The vision shown on the DSD was black. Daniel knew Elizabeth was still dreaming only because he could hear her sobs.

"Listen to me, Elizabeth, we'll meditate together. I know this is a strange place, but there is nothing to worry about. If anything bad starts to happen, I'll just wake you up."

"Do you…do you promise?" she asked between sobs in her childlike voice.

"I promise." Daniel smiled unconsciously. "Why don't you imagine we are in a jungle or at a beach? Then open your eyes, and once we are there, we can explore it together. I can even teach you how to fly."

Slowly, the vision came back, and she looked around. She was still in the church, but it was empty, and there was a tense silence.

Everything happened so fast. Daniel was too slow to notice that the colors of the windows were replaced by a strong red. The cross on the altar was upside down. The ringing of the bells was as loud as a plane. The faceless people were back, all of them looking at her.

"*Daniel!*"

Her scream made Daniel's skin crawl. Now Elizabeth's head was on the floor, and she was crying loudly.

"Help me! He is here!"

"What's going on, Elizabeth?"

"Help!"

And that was when Daniel saw it. From the corner of Elizabeth's eye as her head was being held down on the floor. He saw it in the left corner of the DSD and felt a cold chill. A black figure holding her down. He could only see two red dots and what looked like a grin on his face.

"*It's time for church, Ellie.*"

Its voice was deep and like a roar. Elizabeth was facing the pews, and Daniel could see the faceless people open their eyes, but they had eyes everywhere, not just in their heads—their necks, their arms, their fingers, they were everywhere. And all of the eyes observed her.

"No, Father, please!"

"Stop!" Daniel was now trying to yell at that thing.

"Father, please!" Elizabeth's crying voice begged again.

"*The Lord will provide.*"

An evil laugh, combined with the loud ringing of the bells, pierced Daniel's ears. His gaze shifted away from the DSD toward the keyboard as he looked for the "ESC" key, only to find Elizabeth standing in front of him. She was pale and her eyes were closed. Her gas mask and most of the medical cables were on the floor behind her, except for most of the electrodes, which were still connected to her head.

It was if she were looking down at him, though her eyes

were closed. Daniel was petrified, as he could still hear the horrible dream in the headset. A grin appeared on her face, and she smacked her head against the one-way mirror wall. Daniel heard the solid sound and almost fell backwards. The glass was bulletproof, but it did not stop her. She hit it again and again and again.

Do something, Spence.

Something inside Daniel made him react, so he moved back to the keyboard. Now with a clear mind, he pushed the "ESC" button three times.

The dull sound continued as Elizabeth smashed her head against the one-way mirror wall, blood dripping down her grinning face. The image on the DSD was now black, but he could still hear the bells. Suddenly, the door in the back opened, and the two nurses came running in and took Elizabeth back. At first, she was still grinning and not putting up resistance. Daniel could almost swear he saw her eyes were white and without pupils for a second as she woke up. Then she started crying desperately and screaming, "You promised! You promised!" as one of the nurses injected something into her neck. She put up some resistance, her panic strong, until they finally managed to drag her away, closing the door behind them.

A cocktail of fear and confusion flowed through Daniel's body. His heart wanted to jump out of his chest and run away. He turned and saw Dr. Cowen, who was gasping and looked concerned, as well as Dr. Cooper, who had a very serious and somewhat analytical expression on his face.

"Dr. Cooper, I—"

"I know…"

CHAPTER 15

ON THE WAY to Dr. Cooper's office, Daniel felt numb, detached from reality. He wondered, Where had common sense gone? What was he doing only two weeks ago? How much everything has changed…

The elevator ride was quiet, the three men submerged in their own thoughts, until they reached Level 2. Daniel felt as if he was being escorted.

Just then, Kelly and Dr. Shoop walked out of the computer lab and saw them. Daniel exchanged a quick look with them and assumed he did not look too good, judging by Kelly's expression. They rushed into Dr. Cooper's office, closing the door behind them.

"Have a seat, Mr. Spence," Dr. Cooper said in his usual calm voice as he sat down.

"What the hell was that?" The question slipped from Daniel's lips.

"Calm down. Let's go one step at a time. I want you to tell me everything that happened prior to this reaction, including any weird dreams you might have seen," Dr.

Cooper said, leaning forward, hands together resting on the table.

"No," Daniel responded in a serious tone. "Why don't you actually explain yourself for a change?" His fist closed beneath the table. "Is this related to your revolutionary theory about another dimension? Are we in this impossible search, just disposing of people like guinea pigs? How is it that…?" He paused and tried to lower his voice. "How is it that in two weeks here I've seen two of our subjects go nuts?"

"You have no idea what you are talking about, you insolent—"

Dr. Cooper cut Dr. Cowen off with a hand gesture while he kept looking at Daniel.

"That will be all, Viktor. Please give us some time. I'll meet you downstairs."

Daniel felt Dr. Cowen's eyes penetrating the back of his skull, but he did not care. He guessed that was what happened when someone insulted his hero in front of him. A moment later, the door was shut behind him.

Dr. Cooper took a deep breath, and his lips curved into a smile. "It's time for you to know the truth…I've never really needed interns, you know. Temporarily hiring someone seemed wasteful to me, because they would never be fully engaged in whatever I would be trying to prove." He hunched his shoulders and looked down. Then he looked back up, and he smiled again, this smile more honest and humble. "But it was only just recently that I found this wall in my studies that I can't seem to break. So I thought by adding young vibrant minds with innovative ideas, we could find a way through."

Dr. Cooper paused as Daniel listened carefully. "The

behavior of 3-56B, although extreme, is not new for us here at the institute. The common denominator that triggers these behaviors in our different subjects is an emotion that has been with humanity since the beginning of time: fear." The left side of Dr. Cooper's mouth curled up in a half smile, a sad, more defeated expression. "And even though we are partially responsible for them, you and I both know that there is something else, something behind that fear… something that almost seems to have a will of its own." His blue eyes widened slightly.

Daniel felt a cold breeze blowing around his arms and back.

Could he be talking about…?

"You've seen it too, haven't you?" the old man said. "Missing pupils; pale, dry skin, long, dark hair; fingers that are more like long claws; and that uncanny smile that just sticks in your mind."

"So it does exist. That thing that has being hunting me since I got here…is real?" Daniel said with a perplexed voice.

"I'm afraid so. I named it the Dream Keeper." He stood and walked to the bookshelf to his right, keeping talking. "It's hard to define what it is, but it follows a pattern. First, it'll appear in our dreams, so of course we dismissed it as a nightmare. But then it started to appear in the experiments we ran, causing panic and fear in our subjects. But if that didn't work…Well, it seems as if the…creature had access to each subject's past and darkest moments. So, it'll grab those dark memories, and it'll force the subject to go through them again and again, in the most terrifying of ways. Finally, it'll make an appearance, like the one you saw with 3-56B."

Daniel thought of his first experiment and the dream he had, remembering the crooked smile and croaking laugh coming from Alex's throat. Then he connected it with Kelly's experiment and how it went wrong. The uncanny grin and white eyes looking at her for a split second. Finally, the nightmares he himself had had since he started working here. The pieces of the puzzle fit, and they made sense—in the most crazy of ways, of course.

Dr. Cooper returned carrying a small notebook and placed it on the desk. "Based on the fact that its intensity and recurrence increase as we advance, its objective seems clear: to sabotage our research on the Reverie. That's how I knew we were onto something."

"So, this is why you didn't tell me the 'past evidence' before. You wanted me to see it for myself, just like you wanted me to see the first experiment through. You wanted me to see it; otherwise, I wouldn't believe it."

"Precisely. I needed you to go for a short walk in my shoes before reaching this…inconvenience." Dr. Cooper paused and took a deep breath.

This is madness. It does not make any rational sense, but everything connects, everything follows a pattern. Part of me still wants to resist the idea, but then again another part of me…

"Dr. Cooper, even though there is a lot of evidence, have you considered the idea that this might just be a consequence of sleep paralysis? Maybe—"

"I understand this is hard to digest, especially as a scientist." His voice was clear and strong. "But do not let your fear of the unknown blind you. Do not make the same mistake that my colleagues in the industry made. Open your eyes, Mr. Spence." Dr. Cooper paused for a second, then spoke again in his natural, soft tone. "Let me show you what I mean. Would you happen to have your dream journal here?"

"Oh yes," Daniel responded, reaching for the small notebook in his pocket. Then he remembered the dream with his first subject that was written in it. He would have preferred if Dr. Cooper didn't know he fell asleep during his first experiment, but there was nothing he could do to hide it now.

"It's okay, I don't have to look at it. I just wanted to make sure you had it with you this whole time. I want you to open the notebook in front of you at the yellow tab. Scroll through and pick whichever dream you want. That is my own dream journal."

Daniel looked at the yellow tab and opened the notebook slowly. He scrolled through and choose a random passage:

September 8, 1987

As I lay down after another turbulent day, my drowsy mind started to drift off. My wife was next to me sleeping, and her calm breathing was a delight to my ears. How lovely it was to have her as a support through all of this. All this pain and confusion. She rolled slightly and moved closer. I tried to grab her hand and realized I couldn't. For whatever reason, my hand was not following my instructions. That's when I realized that it was not only my hand. I tried to move my head to see her, but my head wouldn't move. That made me think. My first impulse was to check my pocket watch as a reality check, but I could not move, of course. Then is when it hit me: I hadn't seen my ex-wife in over two decades. So who was next to me? The answer, as I'm writing this, is more than obvious, but in the deep drowsiness of my sleep paralysis, it kept sliding away. At the bottom of my closed eyes, there was a small opening. Big enough for me to see the shadow closing in. This was the Dream Keeper territory. Drowsy and confused, not in a lucid dream and not awake either, I was at my most vulnerable. Through the opening I saw how the shadow moved on top of me, crushing my chest and allowing very little air in, choking me. I tried to use all my concentration to move—the slight movement of any part of my body would break this terrible experience—but I was overwhelmed, as I usually am when I get caught in a sleep-paralysis episode. Then to add to my agony, I saw its face through the small opening of my eyes; I saw its pale-white face, her white eyes looking back. Its claws now pressed my chest even more, and I saw its uncanny smile as it fed on my suffering. Since I could not move my body, I focused on one word: "Out." I could spell it in my head, and I repeated it over and over, louder each time. It felt like hours, though it was probably only minutes, until I could finally break free. I woke up sweating, cold, gasping for air, the Dream Keeper gone.

I need to find a solution; otherwise, sooner rather than later it'll have me for good. For now it is late, so I'll give these thoughts more time tomorrow when I have a clear head.

Daniel looked up, speechless, and found Dr. Cooper's small, sad smirk.

"It has been stalking you, too, the same way it stalks me," he finally said.

"It has chased me since the beginning of my research. At first, I assumed it to be a consequence of post-traumatic stress disorder, but as I made more discoveries and progress, I realized that there were just too many connections. It even got more intense as I made more progress, as if it was hiding something. I think I'm onto something big, Daniel, I really do."

Another long pause dominated the room.

"So what now?" Daniel asked.

"Now we are going to work closely together. We'll research the Reverie directly and make it our objective to find out more about the Dream Keeper."

Daniel opened his mouth to reply, then closed it. He remained quiet for a couple of seconds, choosing his next question carefully. "I am…flattered, Dr. Cooper, but why me? Why wouldn't you use Dr. Cowen or Dr. Shoop, who have being here longer? Or even Kelly? I've only being here for around a month."

Dr. Cooper spoke softly, a small half smile drawn on his face. "You are not going to like what you hear. But I won't lie to you, so are you sure you want to know?"

"Yes. Tell me."

"It's because of your disturbed past. My research has shown that people who go through traumatic events, especially in their childhood, experience a stronger response from the Dream Keeper. Now, as for the reason—well, I believe it's easier for me to show you than to tell you," Dr. Cooper said as he dragged back the notebook from Daniel, closed it, and walked toward the bookshelf.

"Show me?" Daniel asked, following him with his eyes.

"Yes, Mr. Spence, I want you to see everything. You are not the only one with a disturbed past. In fact, you are going to have a very peculiar subject for your next experiment. Of course, all of this needs to stay confidential. Don't tell any of the other researchers. I would like to avoid unintended friction." He slid the book in and went back to the desk but didn't sit down.

Daniel understood that the meeting was over and stood up too.

"Get some sleep. We have a long night ahead of us. Let's meet on Level 4, Room 4D, by seven thirty p.m. tonight."

Daniel intended to protest, but Dr. Cooper raised his hand. "I'm sure you have a lot of questions, but I just dropped a lot of information. Sleep on it and bring all your questions tomorrow. I hope you don't mind working on a Saturday night."

"Not at all. I want to get to the bottom of this." Daniel wanted to discuss more, to find out more, but knew he'd have to wait. So he headed toward the door, but before opening it, he looked back and asked, "Who is the next subject, Dr. Cooper?"

The old man smiled and responded in his calm voice, "It's me, Mr. Spence. I'm your next subject."

CHAPTER 16

A SOFT KNOCK on the door broke the silence that had dominated Daniel's room for the past hour. He lay in his bed, wondering, questioning every single detail of his last meeting with Dr. Cooper. As exhausted as he was, he could not shut off his thoughts, so he just lay there.

The knock came again, this time louder.

"Daniel, it's me, Kelly."

Daniel sat up and, after a long pause, unlocked the door from his bed. The white light from the hallway filtered in and illuminated his room, followed by Kelly's silhouette.

"Were you sleeping?"

"No."

She closed the door behind her and turned on the light. Daniel looked up, squinting to avoid the brightness.

Kelly looked at him with a worried expression. "Is everything okay?"

She sat next to him. Daniel heard Dr. Cooper's soft voice in his head: *Of course all of this needs to stay confidential. Don't tell any of the other researchers.*

"Yeah, it was just a long night. What time is it?"

"It's nine thirty in the morning. I had a late shift, but I saw you in the hallway, and…Well, I just came to check in," Kelly said, shifting positions. "What happened?"

What happened? You really want to go over everything that happened? Well, I don't even know where to start. Should I start with my subject going loony and trying to break the bulletproof one-way mirror wall with her head, or the creepy smile she gave me? Or the ethics behind this whole shit show? Or how about the conversation with Dr. Cooper? How, according to the brightest psychologist in the world, there is an alternate dimension we visit when we sleep? Oh and he likes to call it the Reverie. You know, to add some drama to it. Or maybe I could try to explain that there is a creature in this new dimension that apparently has been with humanity since the beginning of time. Even better, the creature has a peculiar taste for researchers at The Cooper Institute, because of the focus on this new dimension. Actually, let's just go with I'm here because I had a fucked-up childhood and apparently that triggers this monster even more…I don't know, Kelly, where should I start?

"Things are complicated, that's all. There isn't much I can say yet."

"What does that mean? You clearly look like shit. It's the experiment you were working on, isn't it? Something happened. Tell me. Maybe I can help."

"Stop!" Daniel said harshly. He paused to control his voice, then carried on. "Please just stop. I have a lot on my mind, and I need to rest. It's just too much right now."

Kelly remained silent and just looked at him. Daniel kept his eyes on the floor in front of them. She moved closer and slid her hand onto Daniel's face, shifting it toward hers. They were close now, really close; her touch on his unshaven cheek felt soft and nice. He looked in her hazel eyes, and for the first time since they met, Daniel saw a completely different expression on her face. One of caring. For a moment, all of Daniel's thoughts, questions, and worries were replaced by a vision of them kissing right there.

"I know the feeling. I've been there too. Get some rest. We can talk about it tomorrow when you feel better."

She let go, stood up, and walked out of the room, closing the door behind her.

Daniel sat there for a long time, thinking of that touch. Part of him wanted to follow Kelly, embrace that touch and forget about everything. But slowly all his troubles came back to him, filling his head with tormenting questions and doubts. There were too many things going on right now to even consider doing something like that. Besides, wouldn't that complicate things even more?

You are damn right it would, Spence. Keep it in your pants. Besides, you heard the boss. You should not be sharing information with anyone.

But her touch, her expression, her softness... These were things Daniel hadn't experienced since he got there. At this point, he was going crazy with everything that had been going on, so taking a break wouldn't kill anyone, would it? But was she thinking the same way? Or was she just being empathetic?

"I can't deal with this right now," he said out loud to the empty room as he turned off the light and lay back in his bed.

It was less than five minutes later when a knock on the door made Daniel jump out of bed. Knowing who it was, he opened the door and saw Kelly. Without a word, she walked in and kissed him hard. Her lips were even softer than her touch, and with that she sealed away all his worries—at least, for the time being. Yes, he would have time for that later.

He embraced her, too, holding her head tight against his. Daniel pulled her in, feeling her body against his. She ran her nails over his neck as she kissed him again and again. Then she bit his lower lip, which made his manhood grow and was now pressing tightly against her.

Daniel lifted her up off the ground as Kelly placed her arms around his neck, sinking her nails into his back, producing an irresistible combination of pain and pleasure. He dropped her at his bed and started to kiss her neck and heard her low moan, so he kept going down as he unbuttoned her shirt, kissing and biting his way toward her breasts. Daniel slipped one hand around Kelly's back and unbuttoned her bra as he slowly slid his lips across her breast. She bit his ear and licked it slowly, making Daniel shiver in a wave of pleasure. With the tip of his tongue, he licked around her breast first, then slowly up to her nipple. Her moans were louder now as he sucked it and grabbed the other breast with his right hand, squeezing it softly and circling the nipple with his middle finger. She twisted on her back in pleasure and pressed Daniel's head against her breast, moaning and biting her lower lip.

Daniel caressed her sides, feeling every inch of her soft skin. Then he used his left hand to unbutton her pants as he switched to her other breast and sucked it hard. His right hand was now on top of her wet panties, and he massaged the area slowly. His left hand moved toward her butt cheek and squeezed it. She twisted again, but now it was her turn.

With a movement of her hips, they both rolled over, and she was on top. She kissed him hard and slid her tongue into his mouth, then went for his neck and bit him as he made a low growl. He pulled her hair back and tried to kiss her, but she stopped him. As she kept her lips an inch away from his, she smiled, enjoying the tease. Daniel tried to kiss her, but she held him down, smiling. He smiled back and slid his fingers into her panties, feeling her completely and finding her clit. Her smile shifted to a loud moan as he touched her slowly.

Now it was she who was craving him, but he kept his distance. It was his turn to smile. She pulled back, biting her lower lip as Daniel kept massaging her. She took off his pajama shirt and kissed him on her way down. He was hard and craving her touch. So she moved back and took off his boxers. Daniel could still see her breast in the dark room as her bra slipped off.

Kelly held Daniel firmly and felt his body tense. She looked up and saw his eyes and how they begged. Oh, how they begged…She went down on him slowly, teasing him at the base. He groaned loudly, grabbing her breast as she tasted him.

Then with a quick move, Daniel grabbed Kelly by the hips and dragged her lower body toward his head. He quickly took off her pants and panties and brushed his tongue over her clit, sending an electric charge full of pleasure to her brain, making her moan loudly as she licked him too.

After a bit, Daniel felt he was close, but he wasn't done yet. He carried Kelly and dragged her to face him. His lips found hers, and they kissed for a long time while they rolled, and now Daniel was on top.

She grabbed him and led him in. Daniel went in with

full force. It was as if everything that happened the night before was a distant nightmare, and the only thing that mattered now was Kelly, him, and this moment of perfect pleasure. He moved in and out, slowly at first and faster as Kelly's moans filled the room, music to his ears. He went in faster, harder, and felt her nails clawing his back.

With a shift of her hips, they both rolled, and now she was on top. That was when Daniel felt it coming again. As she moved faster, riding him like no one had before, he felt he was about to explode.

He pulled her hair and brought her forward, kissing her deeply, feeling her body connected to his. Wave after wave of pleasure bombarded his brain. She started to shake and moan as they kissed. Every inch of her screamed with pleasure as the tension was released and they both came at the same time.

As Kelly lay on top of Daniel, they both gasped for air.

He was sweating and still gasping when he tried to speak. "That was un— "

But she shot up her hand to stop him speaking. Daniel laughed. He felt her hand cover his mouth and nose. Before he realized it, she was squeezing him hard, allowing very little air to come in. He grabbed her hand and tried to move it. Maybe she was too excited and just oblivious. But he felt a cold arm instead, and that was when he realized her whole body was cold—too cold to be normal, too cold to be human.

He tried to scream but couldn't. Her hand was now the size of his face, with sharps claws sinking into his flesh, sending pain signals to his brain. Through one eye, and even in the dark, Daniel could see two white spheres looking back at him, and he panicked. It approached Daniel's side and whispered in his ear in an almost metallic, high-pitched voice,

"*Leave now.*"

He woke up screaming and gasping for air. The creature, the Dream Keeper, was gone, a headache and a strong sense of nausea having replaced it. He felt ill and dizzy on his way to the bathroom, and that was when he realized his boxers were wet too. He puked and sat in the shower trying to recover from the terrible night. After a while, Daniel stepped out and looked at himself in the mirror. He looked for marks or scars but found none, so he went back to bed. He sat on the side of the bed, fatigued and rubbing his face. That was when he saw his dream journal on the night table, and after a bit of hesitation, Daniel grabbed it and started writing.

CHAPTER 17

DANIEL LEANED ON one of the elevator walls and yawned. The door opened on Level 4. He stepped out without much care and realized the hallways had all the lights off. The door shut behind him and left him in a sea of darkness. After blinking multiple times and adjusting to the lack of light, he saw the red lights above each door in the hallway. Daniel walked slowly, keeping one hand on the wall. After a few steps, he saw there was some white light glowing from one of the doors toward the left. Before he proceeded, the thought that this could be a dream crossed his mind.

If this is another one of the creature tricks, then I ought to at least be prepared this time. If only I knew how…

Daniel reached the door and slid his key into the lock. Surprisingly, it opened, so he went in. The room inside reassembled the Receiver room that Elizabeth used, with the medical chair in the center. Except there was a small desk with a rolling chair, and a screen next to the wall on the right. Daniel recognized the DSD keyboard on the desk. Dr. Cooper was bending under the screen. The old man turned around, stood up, and smiled.

"Good evening, Mr. Spence, how was your sleep?"

"Good evening, Dr. Cooper," Daniel said as he walked into the small room. "Let's just say it wasn't the best. Mind if I ask, why are the hallway lights off?"

"I'm sorry to hear that." Dr. Cooper took off his glasses and started to clean them. "This area is technically restricted. In fact, I added your key code to Level Four and this room after our meeting this morning. I do that to avoid unnecessary attention. I do believe I mentioned my concern for confidentiality from this point on." He put his glasses on a small table next to the medical chair.

Daniel remembered his conversation with Kelly last night—or was it really Kelly? He didn't even know if he saw her. He was not sure of anything anymore.

"Yes, you did," Daniel responded, pushing the memory away.

"And I'm sure you are eager to start. After all, I believe you've gone through a lot of trouble to get where you are now." Dr. Cooper hunched and looked down for a second with a sort of lost look on his face. Then he looked back up and took a deep breath. "Very well, then, let's begin. That's where you'll be seated," he said as he sat down on the medical chair and started to place the electrodes on his head. "I was just installing the screen when you walked in. Feel free to take notes."

"Wait, are you just going to sleep with the electrodes? What about all the medical equipment? What if something like what happened to Elizabeth happens to you, Dr. Cooper?"

The old man laughed deeply. "I'm not an amateur, Mr. Spence. Don't worry, but know this: we will have an encounter with the Dream Keeper today. So be prepared."

He put on the gas mask and leaned back in the chair.

Daniel looked at the keyboard and the small mirror next to it, a bit undecided as to what to do.

The old man has become a little reckless lately. I should try and object; I should try and get an explanation first. I should, but…just say it, Spence: you don't want to. Because you want to know the truth, you want to understand what's behind all of this. What's behind the creature that has tormented you and so many others here at the institute. You want to prove this theory, because as crazy as it sounds, even with a minimal chance of it actually being true, so many doors will open. So many new questions could be asked and discoveries made. So now you just need to be brave and jump in.

He pressed the on button, then looked at Dr. Cooper, who was seated facing him with his eyes closed. Before he could think anything else, Dr. Cooper opened one eye, raised his hand, and gave him a thumbs-up. Daniel smiled, gave him a thumbs-up back, pressed the "SLEEP" button, and observed the readings on the EEG. In a matter of minutes, Dr. Cooper was ready, so Daniel administered the second gas by pressing "REM." He put on the headset, leaned back in his chair, and waited.

Dr. Cooper was not joking when he said he wasn't an amateur. In a matter of minutes, a clear image appeared on the DSD. Daniel leaned forward and saw that, in the dream, Dr. Cooper was seated in an exact copy of his office. His first action was to check his silver pocket watch, which showed the time to be…

Daniel focused on the watch and realized it was not working. In fact, it didn't look like a normal watch. Instead of two hands it had five, one moving clockwise very fast, then two others moving counterclockwise at the same speed as the first. One stayed marking five, and one went backward and forward between six and eight.

"Mr. Spence?"

Daniel heard the old man's voice through the headset and almost jumped.

"Yes, Dr. Cooper? Are you lucid?"

"Indeed I am," he said, closing the watch and placing it on the table.

"So, you knew thanks to your pocket watch."

"Yes. Why don't we look at it again?" Dr. Cooper opened the watch, and Daniel saw a completely different thing. Now there were three hands, each going backward and forward, one between twelve and one, the other between one and two, and the last one between five and nine.

"This is my token. There are specific triggers that lucid dreamers can use to know if they are dreaming. Time is a great one, as you can see here. It does not work as it does in our dimension, so I formed a habit of checking my watch as much as possible each day. Before I do a new activity, I check it, and it will tell me if I'm dreaming or not."

Daniel looked at the sleeping man seated in front of him. One thing was certain: the old man never stopped amusing him. "That's very clever, Dr. Cooper."

"Ha, not really. It's just one of many techniques. Now, let's get going. We have a lot to do."

He grabbed the watch, placed it back in his lab coat, and went toward the door of his office.

As the door opened, Daniel saw a bright light coming from outside. Dr. Cooper stepped out into a green open field. There were small valleys, and the sky was a bright blue with a strong sun.

"Welcome to the Reverie, Mr. Spence."

Daniel was baffled by the sharpness and the color of the dream—very different to what he saw with Elizabeth.

"First, a quick recap," he said as he walked down the valley. "The mind and the brain are two separate entities. When we sleep, our mind manifests in a different dimension, which is processed by our brains as dreams. I named it the Reverie. You also know that there is a sort of creature that manifests whenever there is research done. And we also discussed the appearance of this creature, and how it's linked to fear somehow. Today I would like to show you the rules I've learned from this place and discuss future actions."

Dr. Cooper paused, bent backwards to stretch his back, then grabbed a wooden walking stick that appeared to his right.

"The basic concept behind everything is that awareness equals control, and control equals power. If you reach awareness in your dream, you can start to control it and shape it to your will. There are different levels of awareness, and it requires practice and good habits to reach the highest one, but do not worry, Mr. Spence. That's what I'm here for."

He stopped again and looked up at the clear sky. "Now, the first law that I've set is that time behaves…differently here."

The sun, which was right in the center of the sky, started to move back toward the east. The movement was slow at first, but it increased in speed until it hid behind two mountains, taking all the sunlight with it. A full moon appeared in the west, bringing with it a set of beautiful stars, and together they generated a soft, white glow. But its appearance was brief, as it sped through the sky and hid in the east. The sun appeared in the west and crossed the sky, faster than before, and hid again in the east. The moon followed it, and the cycle repeated itself again and again, each time at a faster phase. Daniel observed the phenomenon, hypnotized by both its beauty and fantastic feel.

In a matter of seconds that could have easily been a couple hundred days in Dr. Cooper's dream, the sky stopped again with the sun right in the center. The old man looked down and started his walk on a paved path that led to a small walled city.

"That's how time works here. It is both malleable and disconnected with this reality. What I mean by that is that it could be a thousand years, and I and what surrounds me will not be affected. The only thing that will affect it is my will to change it. I only possess that will because I'm aware that I am in a different dimension. See how everything connects?"

"Yes…I'm baffled, Dr. Cooper," Daniel said. "This is impressive. I've heard of lucid dreaming before, but seeing how it works with such clarity, I almost feel like I'm in the dream myself."

Dr. Cooper laughed. "And you've seen nothing, my friend. Hopefully, in the near future we will switch places, but that is a conversation that we should have later. I'm afraid we don't have much time."

He walked through the gates of the walled city and entered a small plaza with a fountain in the center. There were kids running around, people walking, and merchants yelling. The whole scene appeared to be from the Middle Ages.

"The second law is that we are not alone when we dream. There are other beings around us that make our experiences more rich. Now, what or who they are is a question I can't yet answer. For now, let's refer to them as the Natives. They can be anyone, from random people, to close friends and even objects and animals. Everything here in the Reverie has the potential to have a will of its own."

He walked next to the fountain, and Daniel could appreciate the three dolphin sculptures spitting water upwards. Then one of them stopped and looked at Dr. Cooper.

"Hey, who are you talking to, old man?" said the statue in a mocking tone.

"Jesus, this guy again. Are you going to mess everything up like last time?" said the other dolphin to the right.

"Quiet, you two. Can't you see he is aware?" said the third, and now the trio scrutinized Dr. Cooper.

The old man stopped in front of them, tilted what seemed to be a hat on his head, and said, "Gentlemen," then carried on.

Daniel observed the bizarre scene with strange fascination. "Who were they?" he asked.

"As I said, Mr. Spence, everything here can have its own personality. Now, whether they are projections of my mind, part of it, or separate entities that exist in this dimension, I can't tell. From what we know, they could be other people dreaming as well. If my hypothesis is correct, the Reverie could very well be a shared space where your mind goes while you sleep. This is why I avoid confrontation with anyone or anything here. It is always good to be respectful, no matter to who or what."

"I see...But with your level of awareness, could you potentially change or influence the Natives?"

Dr. Cooper stopped his walk next to a wagon shop, turned around, and raised his hand toward the three-dolphin fountain.

"Indeed I can," he said, and Daniel saw how the fountain vanished. "But I prefer to avoid it. You don't want to call unnecessary attention to yourself."

While Dr. Cooper said this, Daniel realized that the whole plaza, which had been full of life seconds ago, was now quiet. Everyone was looking at Dr. Cooper. The old man looked around, ignoring the looks, turned and carried on.

"There is only one being that I cannot control."

"The Dream Keeper," Daniel said.

"Yes, but let's save that topic for later. There are still a couple of things I want to show you, and I don't want to attract any…unnecessary attention."

He walked down an alley, and Daniel felt he was in an old city in Europe, surrounded by stone buildings.

"There are different types of Natives. I separated them into three groups depending on their level of awareness: low, medium, or high." He took a left and was now in a larger plaza in the shape of an oval with gigantic statues in the middle of generals on horses. There were a lot of people walking around, and the sun filled the space with warm sunlight.

"Now, let's see…Ahh, perfect." Dr. Cooper walked toward a man who looked like he was homeless who was sitting on the ground in the street. He was drawing a beautiful painting of a boat on an ocean. As Dr. Cooper got closer, Daniel could hear mumbling over the loud background noise of the street.

"…She comes when she wants. She protects what is hers. From the thieves from out there…"

"Mr. Ollman, how's your evening so far?"

The man looked up. He was wearing a hat, and his clothes had holes in them. His face was dirty, but he seemed composed and well. He recited what seemed to be a poem in a loud, enthusiastic way.

Evening, sir,
I believe today is well,
but tomorrow that will change.
The balance will soon shift,
and what you seek,
you will find.
Yet, nothing comes without a price
Unless you are ready to be raided
But do not worry, your successor will
Soon be awakened from her sleep.

Dr. Cooper bowed his head and carried on walking toward the right side of the plaza, toward a set of columns that supported the stone overhangs above. "That is a low-awareness Native. They are usually in their own world doing their thing, and almost always they don't make any sense. They could speak to you for an hour and nothing would make sense."

They were now walking under the stone overhang with the columns toward their left. "Remember the dolphin stones we encountered? Well, I could say that they're probably medium-awareness Natives. Essentially, the more sense they make, the more aware they are. They knew who I was, they remembered me from a previous dream, and they also knew I was a visitor who was 'aware.' Finally, they concluded that my level of awareness was high enough to present a 'threat.' Awareness is control, control is power."

Daniel paid close attention to each word, consuming it like it was food for thought. He was so invested in the conversation that he jumped when he heard a low voice from behind.

"Why are you talking to yourself?" the voice asked, and Dr. Cooper turned around. A tall black man wearing a long black leather jacket was behind him. He wore glasses and had his hair neatly parted to the right. It took Daniel a couple of seconds to notice the indent in his forehead, which was the shape of a closed third eye.

"Ah, Philemon. Perfect timing."

"You know you should not be around like this. It's dangerous. You should go to your Core now. And what did we say about the treatment of other natives? What was that all about with the dolphin brothers? You might attract unwanted attention."

Daniel noticed then that the man was speaking, but his mouth wasn't moving.

Telepathy.

"Oh my dear old friend, I'm afraid I can't talk right now, I'm in a bit of a hurry. Don't you worry about me," Dr. Cooper said as he placed an arm on the tall man's shoulder. "I'll be fine."

"Who is that, Dr. Cooper?" Daniel asked in a low voice.

Suddenly, the third eye on the man's forehead opened. With a yellow iris, it looked straight into Dr. Cooper's eyes, and Daniel suddenly felt goose bumps that started on the back of his neck and ran down his back. Dr. Cooper took his hand back and placed them both behind him.

"I sense a third voice. So, you were actually talking to someone else."

Dr. Cooper remained quiet for a second, and Daniel could feel the tension in the air.

"This is quite a discovery, Philemon. So, you can hear Mr. Spence and what he says to me?" Dr. Cooper said with an intrigued tone.

"I can sense a third presence in your head, but I can't quite decipher what he is saying. I just know it's not your thoughts. What are you up to, Henry?" Philemon scrunched his forehead and kept his gaze on Dr. Cooper.

"I see." Dr. Cooper placed his hand on Philemon's forearm. "As always, you've been of great help, my friend. I'll be going to my Core now. Take care."

"No, Henry, what you are…?" But Philemon's voice became garbled. His face and body, together with the rest of the objects and people, seemed to be wrapped and pulled, leaving a distorted, uncanny image. The distortion was slow at first and increased in speed with time, until the whole scene went black and dead silent.

Seconds later, Dr. Cooper was standing in the middle of a large lobby, which seemed to be of a large Victorian house. There was beautiful marble with gold ornaments and statues. Leading up from the lobby, the welcoming center stairs had gold handrails. It was full of natural sunlight, which filtered in from the windows and gave a golden hue to the space.

On second look, Daniel noticed a familiar face: a little girl of around six years old with curly blond hair and strong blue eyes sat on the third step. She looked up and smiled, and Daniel smiled back instinctively.

"Not now," Dr. Cooper said in a dry voice, and the little girl's smile disappeared. She stood up and ran up the stairs, while Dr. Cooper carried on toward one of the doors on the first level.

"Who was that, Dr. Cooper?" Daniel asked, trying to remember where he had seen her before.

"Just another Native, Mr. Spence," the old man said as he opened the door into a small space. There was a cushion chair facing a large window, next to a small lamp, on top of which seemed to be a night table. He sat and stared outside. A glass of what appeared to be bourbon appeared in his hand.

"So, I'm assuming Philemon was a high-awareness Native. But he could also detect my presence. Is that a normal? He seemed concerned about you."

"Philemon and I go way back—back to the beginning of my journey as a lucid dreamer. He was a powerful guide who taught me a lot of things and gave me advice and guidance about this dimension." He sipped his bourbon and wiggled the glass in his hand. "I've never seen him look through me and find either Dr. Cowen or Dr. Shoop like he did with you. But regardless, I'll give more thought to that later."

Dr. Cooper moved his hand toward his forehead, and it seemed as if he pulled something out of it. Seconds later, Daniel saw what looked like a shiny sort of viscous gas in the old man's hand. In it, he could see some letters floating in and out, and a face or two that he could not understand. The hand let go of the strange gas, and it floated forward, before taking off to the left.

"Now, as you saw, high-awareness Natives seem to have

their own thoughts, personalities, perspectives, desires, and motivations both good and bad, and they even seem to have cognitive abilities. They also possess a degree of power, thanks to their strong awareness. As I said before, in the other dimension, awareness is control, control is power."

"But if they are just projections of our mind, why bother to speak with them?"

"Well, that's a bit egocentric. Truth is, we don't really know what the Natives are. They could be projections of our mind, but they might also be independent beings. Speaking to them is like talking to a local in a foreign country: they can give you directions and guidance."

"I see." Daniel rubbed his face with his hands. "What happened at the end, before coming to this house?"

"Oh, that was me simply teleporting here." He gestured with his hand to the space. "This is my Core, Mr. Spence."

"I'm assuming your Core is sort of your residence here in the Reverie."

"Yes. Everyone has a Core. In it are all of the things related to you—your thoughts, memories, and things you forget, hobbies, everything. It is your personal space in this dimension."

Dr. Cooper drank a bit more of his bourbon and kept staring at the window. Dawn had taken over, and now all the trees surrounding the house were slowly losing their color to the blueish darkness. That was when Daniel saw it, the black silhouette of what seemed to be a tall woman. She just stood there, and Daniel moved closer to the DSD to see who it was.

"Dr. Cooper, someone is outside."

"Oh yes. It has been following us since we made it to

that plaza," Dr. Cooper said in a calm voice. "We both know what that is."

An imaginary ice cube slid down Daniel's spine. "What are we going to do?"

"There is nothing for us to do yet." Dr. Cooper stood up, left the empty glass on the table, and walked down the hall. "Let me show you one last thing. Apparently our time is about to run out."

He stopped in front of another door, opened it, and went in. This room was very dark—to the point where it was impossible to tell where the floor, walls, or even ceilings were. Everything was submerged in a thick darkness except for spots of lights to each side that extended beyond Dr. Cooper's view. It seemed to be an art display, but the fact that the surfaces of the room were not visible gave the impression that everything, including Dr. Cooper, was floating. He went down between the two rows of displays at a fast pace. Daniel could see a typewriter, a small pair of girl's shoes, and further along, something less malleable—a floating sort of plasma of a strong white color.

Dr. Cooper stopped in front of a familiar painting. "Remember this?"

"That's the painting from your office," Daniel said, staring at the weird creature that sat on the woman's belly, followed by the black horse with white eyes, peeking from behind the curtains.

"It's called "The Nightmare," by Henry Fuseli, and was painted in 1781. What do you think?"

"It's creepy," Daniel said, and Dr. Cooper laughed.

"Indeed it is. Well, my belief is that our friend Henry was trying to represent an encounter with the Dream

Keeper. The little demon sitting on the woman's belly is called an incubus. Essentially, it's a demon that attacks and rapes its victims at night. Sound familiar?"

"How did you know?"

"Everything you've felt I probably experienced too." Dr. Cooper took a deep breath. "Dismissing it as an effect of sleep paralysis is the easy way out. But considering this is another dimension, how can we confirm that this isn't real? We could even go further and look into some of the details of the painting. Like the diary on the night table, or a corner of what seems to be a mirror. Now, to the normal public, they may seem like common objects, but to me as a lucid dreamer, they are tokens, key in becoming lucid. How can we—?"

"Dr. Cooper?"

"It's here."

CHAPTER 18

THE ROOM WAS filled with tension. Dr. Cooper walked backwards slowly as the painting and other objects in the space faded away into a darkness so thick, it seemed to be a gas clouding the vision.

"I guess it's time to wake up, Daniel," Dr. Cooper said in a calm voice as he extended his hands forward in a sort of martial arts position.

Daniel quickly rushed to the keyboard and pressed the "ESC" button. The sound of the sleep gas flowing gradually stopped for a moment. The room was in complete silence. The DSD was now pitch-black.

"Dr. Cooper?" Daniel asked with hesitation.

Instead of a response, Daniel heard white noise and static. Soon after, a new image appeared on the DSD: a infinite hallway, identical to the ones on every floor of the institute. The gray tones were accentuated by the large fluorescent troffers. Further in stood a white figure.

"Shit. Dr. Cooper, you need to wake up now. The Dream Keeper—it's here!" Daniel yelled. He got up and shook the old man, without response.

Suddenly, some of the lights in the hallway shown by the DSD started to fail. They went on and off and flickered randomly, especially further in, where the creature was located. The white body, which seemed to be an inch long on the DSD, disappeared when the light on top turned off. A couple of seconds later, the body appeared again, this time closer.

Daniel, who was in a state of panic, heard what seemed to be Dr. Cooper's voice a little more clearly over the static.

"…Up…Observ— …help…" were his last words before the static took over, louder than before.

The body was getting closer by appearing and disappearing. Daniel saw Dr. Cooper's arms extend forward, with his hands open. The creature made it to about ten feet from Dr. Cooper when a glass wall appeared between them. The old man's arms were tensed forward, shaking, his palms facing the creature. The Dream Keeper disappeared and appeared again right behind the wall. Daniel saw the white disproportionate body in detail now, the long extremities with large fingers that ended in sharp claws. Its upper body was slightly tilted to the right; its head stood straight with that uncanny smile on its face; its white eyes focused straight ahead, on Dr. Cooper…and Daniel.

For a moment, the creature just stood there. It almost seemed as if it was savoring the moment, enjoying having cornered its prey. The static suddenly stopped, and thick silence took over both dimensions.

"No…" Dr. Cooper whispered.

The creature raised a claw and touched the glass wall, which crumbled. The lights from the hallways started to burn off as Dr. Cooper fell to his knees. For a moment, everything went dark and the silence persisted. Daniel stood up and tried to shake Dr. Cooper again—harder this time—but still without success.

"Come on, old man, you need to get out of there! Why are you still asleep without the gas?" he yelled.

The sound of a ragged breathing filtered through the headset. Daniel went back to the DSD and saw Dr. Cooper's shadow on the floor. The light came from behind, and slowly Dr. Cooper turned around. From the back of his left eye, he saw the Dream Keeper standing right behind him.

"Come on, get it over with," Dr. Cooper said loud and clear.

"Daddy?"

A childish, sweet voice suddenly interrupted the whole scene. Far ahead in the darkness stood the silhouette of a kid with long curly blond hair. A high-pitch metallic voice started to croak again and again. It almost sounded as if the Dream Keeper were laughing.

"Finish it!" Dr. Cooper yelled, fixing his gaze on the floor.

"Daddy, no!" the little kid screamed, and ran toward Dr. Cooper.

The metallic laughter was louder now. The Dream Keeper grabbed Dr. Cooper's head by the chin with its claws and forced him to look up at the little girl, who ran toward him, crying.

"No, please stop it," Dr. Cooper begged.

Just when the girl was about to reach them, two sharps claws pierced Dr. Cooper's throat. The little girl stopped her run and yelled. She cried as Dr. Cooper's blood spilled forward. A watery sound came as he tried to gasp for air. The two claws slid backward, and Dr. Cooper fell face forward into a pool of blood.

For a moment, the only thing Daniel could hear was Dr. Cooper's last gasps for air. The little girl disappeared, and the image from the DSD started to fade. That was when he saw how the creature appeared back on screen. Its pale feet approached the dying old man. It bent over and inspected his body. Its protruding white eyes finally stopped on Dr. Cooper's own, and now it was looking at the DSD, looking back to another dimension, looking back at Daniel.

What were merely a few seconds felt like hours to Daniel as the two beings exchanged looks. But the emotion he felt wasn't fear. No, for the first time, Daniel looked at this creature with a mix of anger, defiance, and a strange fascination.

"What are you?" Daniel's voice came as an involuntary whisper.

Next to him, Dr. Cooper started coughing uncontrollably. He tried to sit up, fighting the cough and gasping for air. Daniel hurried to help him, but right before he took his headset off, a croaking sound, more metallic than human, spoke, sending a chill down his spine:

"Daniel..."

CHAPTER 19

HE LOOKED BACK at the DSD and saw it was completely dark. Nevertheless, he was certain of what he heard and felt a cold shiver run through his body. His hands were still on the headset when Dr. Cooper's cough brought him back.

"Shit," Daniel said, finally taking the headset off and rushing toward the old man.

"Dr. Cooper, you need to relax. You are back at the institute," Daniel said, grabbing him by the upper back and bringing him forward slowly.

Dr. Cooper's cough slowly stopped, leaving a scared man with wide-open red eyes. Tears rushed down his cheeks, but it was hard for Daniel to know if they were a consequence of the dream or an effect of the coughing fit.

"Are you still with me?" Daniel fetched a cup of water. Dr. Cooper took it in a shaky hand and drank.

The old man stared at the floor as he spoke in his soft voice. "I know that what I'm about to ask is not only selfish but crazy." He looked up at Daniel, and after a couple of seconds where he seemed to be debating something in his mind, he stated, "I need you to become a lucid dreamer.

I've found a way to connect minds and have them manifest together in the other dimension. I'll train you, and together we can face the Dream Keeper and finally get the answers we've been looking for."

Daniel was speechless. What the old man asked was crazy. That creature was already making him, making everyone, miserable. No matter how much he wanted answers, he was not interested. But the worst part was that Dr. Cooper was not necessarily asking; he was demanding in a very subtle way.

What can you say when your boss asks you to do something you don't want to?

"You do it."

His father's voice had returned.

"I...I don't think I can, Dr. Cooper. I've only been here for a month, I don't feel like I have the experience..."

"Your fear is understandable, Mr. Spence, but I'll train you and be with you every step of the way. So, you do not need to worry about experience."

"But what about Dr. Cowen or Dr. Shoop? They've been here longer and are full-time researchers."

"I tried. They both failed. They didn't have the determination and motivation that you do."

Daniel felt trapped. It was as if anything he said the old man would counter. "What are you talking about? I'm just an intern."

"You are more than that. You are special, Mr. Spence," Dr. Cooper answered as he reached into his front pocket. He took out his wallet, opened it, and gave it to Daniel.

Daniel took it and saw a small picture. A little girl with curly blond hair and strong blue eyes stared back. It was the little girl from the dream, and that was when things clicked: she was the same girl as in the picture on Dr. Cooper's desk.

"That's my daughter." Dr. Cooper looked down as he spoke. "Her name was Olivia. She passed away when she was just six years old."

Daniel felt a stone sink in his stomach. "I'm sorry to hear that."

"Thank you," he said, then looked back at Daniel. "She was full of love and curiosity. And quick on her feet too." A sad smile appeared on his face as he hunched over and looked down again. "She left this world too soon. It happened a long time ago, and I was devastated. Only people like you would understand what it is like to lose someone you love unconditionally."

Daniel remained quiet, and Dr. Cooper carried on. "This happened when I was in my late twenties and essentially destroyed my marriage. I threw myself into the only comfort I had left: my research. That's essentially how I became the renowned person I am today." Dr. Cooper cleared his throat and looked back at Daniel. "Why am I telling you this story? I never thought I would see my daughter again. But everything changed when I started my research on dreams. I've reached lucidity and was making constant field trips to what I then called the dreamland. It was on one of those field trips that I saw her again. I was sitting on my porch, taking some mental notes and meditating about the natives, when I saw her. She was just running around, chasing her red ball and laughing like she did when she was alive. Imagine my surprise." He smiled. "After the initial shock, I called for her, and she came and gave me a big hug just as real as the chair I'm sitting in now." A tear slid down his cheek, and he rubbed it away with a finger. "Forgive me. I don't intend to get emotional. It was just… after all those years…you understand."

"I do," Daniel said with bitterness, looking at the floor.

The old man took a deep breath and carried on. "So I started to interact with my daughter more and more. At first, I thought that she was just a projection of my thoughts, of my memories, but the more I interacted with her, the more convinced I was that that was not the case. She was a native, one with a very sharp mind and high awareness. By then, I had already developed the theory of the Reverie. That's when the thought first crossed my mind: What if the Reverie is not just a parallel dimension to ours but also the next step? The place we go after we die…What if our minds somehow manifest there after—?"

"A place we go after we die," Daniel whispered.

"But the strangest thing was that, right around the time I had that realization and wrote down my hypothesis, the Dream Keeper started to appear. That's when the sabotage and stalking and torment began, just like what you saw today. But that only motivated me to move forward. I needed to get to the bottom of this. Sadly, none of my researchers know this or could possibly understand it, because they haven't been through the suffering of losing someone they love who they are not supposed to lose."

"So, that's what you meant when you said you wanted to show me before," Daniel said with a somber voice. "That's why you hired me. Because of what happened to my little brother and my mother."

"Partially, yes. Very few fit the profile I was looking for, but to get someone with your qualifications, experience, and abilities who could eventually understand what I'm trying to prove here and share my motivation…It was too good to be true."

"So, you believe that by becoming lucid and working with you, there is a chance I will be able to see both of them again."

"Potentially, if I'm right. You can help me prove it. Just think about it: if it works, you will see them again; if it doesn't, then I'll give up and move on. I'll state that my hypothesis was wrong and we'll focus on something else."

See them again.

Daniel took a deep breath. "I don't know, Dr. Cooper, this is a lot to digest."

"Just think about it. Why don't you take tomorrow off, considering you've missed the last three Saturdays counting tonight? We can finish this discussion on Monday."

"All right, Dr. Cooper. I'll think about it."

As dawn broke, the first rays of the sun filtered through the large cafeteria windows. Daniel sat staring at his plate of fruit. The institute was usually almost deserted early Sunday morning, but Daniel had too much on his mind to even notice.

I bet you can't reach the bottom.

He looked up at the ceiling, trying to keep his composure.

It has been so long, and yet the scar of losing someone you love unconditionally never really heals. You just sort of learn how to live with the pain and hope one day you see them again. But when the responsibility lands directly on your shoulders, things change. You don't just try to understand the inexplicable;

A. B. Cohen

you instead try to come to terms with the fact that you are the explanation. I am the reason, responsible for their deaths.

Having an opportunity to do the right thing, to be able to apologize face-to-face…It just seems too good to be true, despite the fact that the Dream Keeper will probably be there waiting for me. Yet as humans, the one inexplicable event in our lives is death. I could come to terms with it, but if there is a chance to understand it, to find just the slightest evidence of something after death, the slightest evidence that tells me my loved ones are okay, isn't that worth the risk?

These thoughts came and went in Daniel's head. He decided he was not hungry, so he threw away the fruit and went to his room. As he waited for the elevator, he heard loud voices talking and laughing. He saw Kelly, Dr. Cowen, Dr. Shoop, and two other nurses appear in the corridor, coming back from their night out. Seeing them cracked a small opening in his chest. When was the last time he hanged out with them, hanged out with anyone really?

The elevator doors opened, and he rushed in. Daniel heard the voices approaching, so he pressed the "Closed Door" button repeatedly. The doors closed, and Daniel felt a sense of relief.

"All right, see you all tomorrow," Kelly said as the doors opened again, and she walked in alone.

"Hey." For a second, Daniel could read embarrassment in her face. "We just got back from the bar. We looked for you but couldn't find you."

"I…I was working with Dr. Cooper. He asked me to work overtime today." He tried to push away the memory of the dream he had two nights ago.

They exchanged glances as the doors shut behind them.

158

It was as if Kelly was trying to find answers in Daniel's eyes. Maybe she was trying to find out more about their last encounter, but Daniel looked away.

She looked around, then leaned in to Daniel and whispered, "You know, you still look like shit. Are you gonna tell me what's going on or what?"

Daniel hesitated for a second. He knew he was not supposed to, but he could not help it anymore. There were too many thoughts in his head and too much baggage on his shoulders.

"Want to take a smoke break?"

Kelly half smiled. "I have Camels."

"Perfect." Daniel pushed "Door Open" and they stepped back out.

CHAPTER 20

"So, what's on your mind, Spence?" Kelly said as she lit up her cigarette and offered one to Daniel.

They were walking around the perimeter of the building as the sun came up.

"There is a lot to tell you and not much time," he said as he took the cigarette.

"This feels like déjà vu," Kelly said, taking a puff. "About time you got me up to date."

Daniel took a drag, looked up at the sky, and blew out the smoke, then started. He told Kelly everything, every detail of the Theory of the Reverie, the Dream Keeper, the different rules of this new dimension, everything. Kelly just listened, and Daniel could feel some of the weight he felt on his shoulders lift. The more he talked, the more he wanted to talk, the more he wanted to scream, the more he wanted to laugh about it, the more he wanted to cry about it; because everything sounded so crazy, so absolutely ridiculous and intense. But the worst part was that it could all be true. Hell, now he was almost certain everything was true, and that was what made everything so (*exciting*) scary.

It wasn't until he came to the last set of events and the last request that he hesitated. Yes, he would be violating protocol and disobeying Dr. Cooper if he told her, but that was not what stopped him. He knew that telling Kelly about Dr. Cooper's latest hypothesis would open the door to deeper thoughts, and some inner demons are best left alone.

"Hold on, this is insane! This theory has no scientific basis and makes no sense at all," Kelly said, more frightened than anything else.

Daniel took another puff and remained silent for a couple of seconds. He finally made the decision. "But that's not all. Dr. Cooper believes that somehow the Reverie could actually be a place where our minds manifest after we die."

"What?!"

Daniel went on and explained his latest experiment to Kelly and what he saw in Dr. Cooper's dream. He talked about the old man's daughter and how he was certain it was her.

Kelly took a deep breath. "This is just unbelievable. Dr. Cooper has gone crazy!"

"Yeah, and now he wants me to go with him. He wants to train me, to guide me in becoming a lucid dreamer. He wants us to go to the Reverie together, research it in a sort of field trip."

"Field trip? These are dreams, Daniel, not some forest where you can just go and take samples. I can't deny there might be something else going on, but we've both seen how dangerous it can be. Besides, why you? Why, out of all of us, is he choosing the least experienced one, the intern? Isn't that a bit suspicious?"

"That's the thing…" Daniel took one last drag and

threw the cigarette to the floor. He stepped on it and carried on. "I was chosen to be here for a specific reason." He looked down, then back up at Kelly. "It's because of my past. I went through…traumatic events as a kid. So he believes that makes me stronger. He believes my will to see them again will be a determining factor in defeating the Dream Keeper and moving on with the research. And I"—Daniel took another deep breath—"I believe him."

"You can't be serious. Even if his theory is correct, and his hypothesis is correct, that does not make the Reverie any more safe. We've seen what happens when we push the boundaries there. This is—"

"I know!" Daniel yelled. He felt heat passing down the back of his neck. "I know it sounds crazy. But it's not that simple."

"I can understand that it's hard, but this is just not natural, Daniel. All of this is just too much."

"You think I don't know that? You think I haven't thought of it already? Imagine you get the chance to see your deceased family again," Daniel said, irritated. "Have you ever had anyone close to you die?"

"I haven't, but—"

"Then of course you will not understand. Of course to you I'm illogical, but so what if I am?"

Kelly's expression turned serious. "Daniel, listen to me," she said softy. "I know this is hard, but I just don't have a good feeling about this. It's just not natural to—"

"Oh fuck that! Don't come and tell me what's natural! Was it natural that my seven-year-old brother died while playing a game with me, his older brother? Was it natural that our mother committed suicide because she could not bear living with the pain? Was it natural that she could not speak or comfort me because I was responsible for everything? Tell me, *is that natural?*!"

Kelly looked at him, hurt, but standing her ground. "Why are you telling me this? Why are you telling me everything now?"

That question took Daniel by surprise, so he looked away. Kelly pulled his arm back. "I'm serious. I went to your room Friday night, and you would not dare speak about anything. And now you are just dumping all this information and expecting me to tell you what you want to hear? You might have gone through some tough times, but that does not mean you are right about this."

Daniel stood there as the words slowly pierced his stubborn skull and started to make sense. He calmed down, but as his anger and irritation diminished, another feeling started to take over: sadness.

"I can't understand your position unless I know the full story. Maybe if you tell me what happened, I can understand."

Was that what he was looking for? Kelly made a really good point: Why did he tell her? Why did he violate a direct instruction from his boss and tell her a theory that was so crazy? The only way someone would believe it was if they experienced it, like Daniel did. Was he looking for sympathy? Or did he just need another opinion, one that would bring him back from the craziness of the last couple of weeks? Why?

I bet you can't reach the bottom.

Kelly sat on the asphalt and gestured for Daniel to sit next to her. He followed her and started telling his tale.

"Come on, Ricky, before Mom and Dad wake up," whispered Daniel from the top of his bunk bed.

"I'm coming, I'm coming," Ricky answered in a drowsy voice.

The two boys put on swimsuits, and Daniel opened the window in their room and jumped out. Ricky, who was smaller and seemed more fragile, was hesitant to follow suit.

"It's a bit high," the seven-year-old said with a shaky voice.

"You can do it! Here, this will help," Daniel said as he pushed some dead leaves onto the spot where he landed seconds ago. "There, that will make it softer," he told his little brother, smiling.

Ricky smiled back, then took one more breath and jumped. He landed on the leaves.

"See, it wasn't that bad. Now let's go."

The two boys left the large wooden house and ran down toward the lake. Their nervous giggles bounced off the forest trees surrounding them, and when they reached the edge of the lake, they stopped, as did their laughter. Who would be the one brave enough to test the water temperature?

"You go," Ricky said.

Daniel smiled at him, and with a quick movement of his arm, he grabbed his little brother by the hips, carried him, and jumped in the water. The cold temperature hit their bodies like an electric current.

"Daniel!" Ricky screamed, laughing. "It's so cold!"

"Stop complaining and swim, little one. That will help."

Ricky giggled as they both swam toward the center of the lake.

"Can you walk?" Ricky asked as he dog paddled, struggling to stay afloat.

"Not anymore. We must be close to the center of the lake. Wanna play a game?"

"Yes!" Ricky said, excited, with a sweet smile.

"I bet you can't reach the bottom," Daniel said with a smirk as he tried to stay afloat.

"I...I don't know if I can."

"Sure you can. Here: watch and learn," Daniel said, and dove to the bottom.

For the next few seconds, Ricky waited nervously. It could have been fifteen seconds, but they sure felt like years to the poor kid, until finally his older brother swam back up. Daniel smiled and extended his fist. A handful of greenish mud slipped through his fingers.

"See? Just take a big gasp of air and swim down. Then extend your fist and grab a bit of mud."

"Oh...okay," Ricky said with a frightened voice. "Here I go." He dove to the bottom.

Daniel waited for his little brother, smiling. A couple of seconds had gone by when he saw a couple of bubbles popping at the surface. He waited a bit longer.

"Ricky?" Daniel asked, now worried.

A set of large bubbles came up and popped at the surface. Realizing what was happening, Daniel dove down quickly. A couple of feet below, he saw the silhouette his little brother. He swam toward him, grabbed him, and tried to swim back up but couldn't. Ricky was moving violently, desperate. He looked back down and realized Ricky's leg was entangled in a branch. Even underwater, Daniel could hear his little brother's screams. Panic took over him, and suddenly all of the air escaped his body. He tried to pull again, but it was no good. He swam back

165

to the surface, took another gulp of air, and quickly swam back down. This time, Daniel went for the leg and started to force the thick branches to make an opening. But something was different. He was the only one panicking; his brother wasn't moving.

He swam back to the surface and grabbed another lungful of air. Then he quickly returned to the bottom. With his last bit of strength, he pulled Ricky's leg up. One of his feet started to get stuck in by the mud when finally Ricky's leg slipped through the opening. Then, after a couple of quick jerks, he unburied his foot and swamp back up, bringing his little brother with him.

"Ricky! Ricky!" Daniel yelled as he tried to pull his brother to the surface. He took him by the arm and tried to swim ashore, checking that Ricky's head stayed above water.

It took him a long time, but he finally made it to the shore. He dragged his little brother onto the sand.

"Dad!" Daniel yelled. "Mom!"

Daniel put his brother down and knelt next to him. Ricky was pale and had some blue spots around his mouth and cheeks, but other than that he seemed to be in a sweet slumber.

"Ricky! Ricky!" yelled Daniel as he yanked him backwards and forward, trying to wake him up, trying to get a reaction.

"Daniel!" his father yelled as he ran toward them, followed by his mother. They were wearing their pajamas and were barefooted.

"I'm sorry! I'm sorry! We went to the lake, and Ricky got stuck and..." Daniel stopped as his father knelt beside him.

"Move over, Daniel!" He shoved him to the side as he bent down and pressed his head against Ricky's chest.

Daniel stepped back, and that was when he realized he was crying. He looked up at his mother, who seemed to be in *shock as she watched her husband apply CPR to their son. The sight of his mother was too much to bear, so he looked down, ashamed. He saw Ricky and his father, Robert, pushing his chest again and again in a rhythmical way. The whole scene seemed like a dream, a nightmare, and that was when Daniel saw Ricky's hand, closed in a fist, a handful of greenish mud slipping through his fingers...*

There was silence for a moment. Kelly put her hand on Daniel's back, but there wasn't much else she could do.

"My mother entered a deep depression, so she was prescribed some new pills. Two weeks later she died of an overdose. I guess it was too much for her to have her oldest son murdering his younger brother."

"I'm sorry about your mom and brother," Kelly said in a low voice. "Daniel, it was an accident. You can't keep blaming yourself like that."

"You can say what you want, but that's why I'm still moving forward with the research. Now that there is a chance, even if it's small, to make things right, I'll take it."

Kelly remained quite for a moment. "So, if your decision is final, then why are you telling me?"

Daniel took some time to respond. He knew the answer, but not the right words to explain. "Because if something... happens to me and I don't make it, or I go all crazy, I want someone to understand why."

The cold air of the early morning was doing the talking now, the breeze brushing their faces.

"I'll try to help you in any way I can," Kelly said with half a smile; however, her tone said something different. "But please be careful."

CHAPTER 21

"WELCOME BACK, MR. Spence," Dr. Cooper said.

Daniel slowly opened his eyes. He tried to shield them from the harsh fluorescent light with his hand as a peculiar smell filtered through his gas mask. He lay on a medical chair and could hear his heart beeping thanks to the monitor in the back. The receiver room was quite dull, with white walls and floor, and his reflection stared back at him in a large mirror. Dr. Cooper's voice came from a set of speakers in the ceiling.

"How are you feeling? That was a long one."

"What...what's happening?" Daniel asked as he took off the gas mask and repositioned himself on the bed.

"I'm training you to become a lucid dreamer. We have been doing it for the past couple of days," Dr. Cooper responded patiently. "Just relax for a bit. We woke you up while you were in the deep-sleep stage. Some drowsiness and confusion are expected."

Slowly, the memories started to come back. "What date is it?"

"It is Sunday, June 11, 1995. We've been doing multiple dream sessions each night. I must say I'm impressed, Mr. Spence. No one has ever been able to keep up with such intense training for more than a day or two, and you are a week in. Your determination is admirable."

My family.

That was when Daniel fully remembered. "How close are we, Dr. Cooper? How close am I to becoming a lucid dreamer?"

"It is hard to tell, but we are heading in the right direction."

"Let's go again," said Daniel, looking at his reflection in the one-way mirror wall, knowing Dr. Cooper was on the other side.

"I must suggest otherwise. This would be your fifth session of the night. Most people I've trained only go three times. I'm afraid you are pushing yourself too hard."

I bet you can't reach the bottom.

"No, please, Dr. Cooper, let's go again. I think I'm almost there."

After a couple of seconds, Dr. Cooper said, "All right, one more session. But know that if I see any possible danger, I'm bringing you back immediately."

"Fine," Daniel said. He put on the mask and lay back again. A now-familiar smell flowed in, and slowly the room started to go dark.

Daniel sat on the edge of his bed with his hands on his forehead. He was massaging it, trying to stimulate it somehow. After all these sessions with Dr. Cooper, he could not help but feel groggy. He would also experience really strange dreams like the one he just had. Something about a flying boat with three kids on it that was cruising across the ocean and suddenly took off toward space. But he was already forgetting the dream, so he rushed to the side of the bed and grabbed his pen and dream journal. He opened it and read the poem on the first page like he always did, except this time something was different. Daniel turned to the next page and the one after, confused. Instead of the dreams and thoughts, there were scribbles. He quickly threw it away, as if it were hot metal in his hands.

What the hell?

"Mr. Spe…hear…e?"

Daniel froze and turned around, standing from his bed quickly. The voice seemed to come from an old radio with a lot of static.

"What the hell is going on?" Daniel asked the emptiness of his room. "Dr. Cooper?"

No answer came. Confused, he grabbed his journal again and inspected it in more detail. There were scribbles all over it, without a specific pattern or meaning.

This is not normal. But if this is not normal, there is a reason for that. I'm not crazy, I'm…dreaming.

He looked around, now distrusting everything he saw. Then he started to remember why he was there, what they were doing.

He took a deep breath. "Dr. Cooper, can you hear me?"

Silence. Just before Daniel started to worry, a radio voice with some static spoke back.

"Congratulations, Mr. Spence, you have become lucid."

"Lucid…" Daniel looked around. Everything seemed to be normal, and yet something was off.

"So my journal is actually my token, what triggers my lucidity."

"Essentially. The journal became part of your routine. The idea is that if something in your daily routine is off, then it can trigger questions that can lead to awareness."

"I see, but why is there a poem there too?"

"I had to take precautions in case you didn't really write down your dreams in the journal. After all, I did not really know how committed you were going to be to all of this. So I had something imprinted there that you could still try and read. What is important is that you try to read something, because as you could tell, written words do not exist in this dimension. Just like my pocket watch showed nonsense in my dream before, the written word can't be displayed in the Reverie."

"But why not?"

"We don't know yet. It's just part of the logic of this dreamland. But even if we don't understand it, we can still use it to our advantage."

"I see." Daniel looked around his room again and felt weird. His room was an almost exact replica of the real one. "What should we do now?"

"I think we should start by finding your Core. Along the way, I can show you a couple of tricks in case you need them for self-defense."

"Only a couple?"

"Yes. It'll take a long time for you to be fully aware, and I don't want to push you, Mr. Spence," Dr. Cooper said patiently. "I can teach you more techniques when we visit the Reverie together." He cleared his throat and proceeded.

"Now, I need you to think that behind a door, you can step out into an open field. This is all concentration, so bear with me."

"Think that I'm walking outside? But where?"

"It does not matter. Just try to picture it in your head."

"All right."

Daniel approached the door carefully, opened it, and saw another door, a red one.

"You are not focusing. Try again."

Daniel did, and this time a strong, cold storm blew his hair backwards. He tried to take a peek, but the wind was too strong, so he ended up closing both doors.

"Okay, let's try something else. Try your bathroom door, but I need you to think hard and focus."

Daniel walked over to the other door, took a deep breath, and opened it. There was a lot of light, so it took his eyes a couple of seconds to adjust to the new environment. Once he saw clearly again, he was astonished by a beautiful valley. It was covered in green, with patches of white-and-yellow flowers. It smelled like freshly cut lawn, with a touch of something sweet; the air was warm and nice as the wind blew gently.

No fucking way.

"Language, Mr. Spence."

"What? I did not say anything," Daniel responded defensively, a bit ashamed.

"When you talk in a dream, you are actually thinking instead of talking. That's the way communication works in the Reverie. So you've been thinking you are talking to me all this time."

"Talk about invasion of privacy here," Daniel said as he saw the beautiful fields that extended infinitely.

"All right, let's get going. We don't have much time. I want you to walk. It does not matter which direction."

Daniel walked, and a couple of steps later turned around to see his room, but it was gone now.

This place is freaky.

"Oh, you have no idea."

For the next couple of hours, Daniel followed Dr. Cooper's instructions and learned a couple of new tricks. First, he showed him how to change his environment, go from a sunny valley to thick jungle with a cloudy sky. After practicing for a bit, Daniel got so good at it, he made a very humid forest, to the point where he could see fishes swimming through the thick air.

The second thing he learned was how to project new objects. This consisted of picturing an object in your head and trying to make it appear in the dream. At this, Daniel was not so gifted, and it was some time before he managed to create a long walking stick.

"Okay, I think that should be good enough," Dr. Cooper said as Daniel inspected his new invention. "So tell me, when you were younger, which place was your happy place?"

"Happy place?"

"Yes, a place where you felt secure, and you had a lot of happy experiences."

Daniel thought for a moment. There was a place, but... "I'm sorry. Nothing really comes to mind."

Dr. Cooper remained quiet for a bit, and Daniel thought he might have finally drained the old man's patience.

"Okay, then, let's try this. I want you to close your eyes and imagine you are going somewhere. It does not matter where."

"All right." Daniel took a deep breath and did so. For a while he felt nothing, but slowly but surely he started to feel dizzy, as if the space around him was rocking like a boat. Soon the movement became almost violent, and he felt himself falling backwards, so he opened his eyes. Daniel was mesmerized by what he was seeing: stars, millions of stars, around him as he floated through space at a very high speed. There was a greenish-blue fog, similar to the northern lights, surrounding him. It was as if he were swimming in the Milky Way. Daniel embraced the flight, and now he was laughing and enjoying himself in a sort of psychedelic, never-ending trip.

It could have been an hour later—maybe less, maybe more; it was hard to tell—when he saw the end, his landing spot. It appeared to be a star at first, but it kept getting larger than the others, until Daniel could actually see through it. Now that he was close, he saw it as an opening in the space, and inside he could see trees surrounding a lake from above. He tried to slow down but did not know how, so he covered his head with his arms and hoped for the best. Daniel's body went through the portal, and he immediately felt the change in climate to a cool, sunny space. He approached the ground at high speed and landed like someone jumping and face-planting the ground—not really a dangerous thing to do, but definitely painful.

Hyperventilating, Daniel sat up and rubbed his forehead. It took him some time to reincorporate, but when he stood up and looked around, he immediately recognized the place.

"This is"—Daniel turned to look in both directions—"Onota Lake."

"So this is where it brought you. You must have a connection to this space."

"Well…" He stopped for a second, trying to order his thoughts. "My dad used to have a cabin in the woods around here. We would go there on long weekends."

"Could you describe it to me?" Dr. Cooper asked in the same voice a doctor would use to ask a little kid to describe the pain that has been bothering him the past couple of days.

"I don't remember it superwell, it has been a while. But it basically consisted of a wooden front porch with big, smooth, wooden columns. Inside, we had a small kitchen, and then a large living room. Every wall was made out of timber, except for the back wall, where the chimney was. That one was made out of large black stones. There was…" Daniel stopped halfway through the sentence.

No.

The wooden cabin from his childhood stood just a couple of feet away from him.

"Welcome to your Core, Mr. Spence. I think this is it," Dr. Cooper's calm voice came through. It seemed like ages since he last spoke. "Just remember, if I see any signs of danger, I'm waking you up. Now, what are you waiting for? Go inside," Dr. Cooper finished cheerfully.

Part of Daniel wanted to run inside. Run like he did when he was a kid, calling for his mom, racing Ricky to the couch in the living room. "No running with wet feet, kids," his dad would say every time. The memory drew a smile to Daniel's face, but a sad one: so many things had changed since then.

"Would my family be inside?" he asked in an innocent little kid's voice.

"There is only one way to find out." The old man's voice sounded like the voice of a father guiding his young son through a new and scary experience.

Daniel hesitated for a couple of seconds and then walked up the stairs. He placed his hand on one of the columns and felt how smooth it was; yes, this was real, this was his home. Daniel took a deep breath and went inside.

Both the kitchen to his left and the living room to the front were exactly how he remembered them. The chimney, the two leather couches, the rocking chair, the center glass table all on top of a rug, the central stairs that went to the second level, everything was there. But what impacted Daniel the most was the smell: the smell of trees and breeze and wood and fire all combined.

"This is…unbelievable."

He went up the stairs and turned left to find his room. There was the bunk bed on one side and a closet on the other. There was a large window with open curtains, the one he and his little brother used to escape from their parents' fierce rules, to go explore.

"I call the top bed!" Ricky's voice bounced in Daniel's head, or was it in the room? It was hard to tell now. Nevertheless, a smile appeared on his lips. They had this game called The Boat, which consisted of a giant boat that traveled through space and time. They visited so many places.

Daniel snapped out of it and left the room. Down the

hallway, he saw the door of his parents' room. He walked over and at first he just stared at it. Then he knocked. He and his brother did not have permission to go inside when the door was shut, so he hesitated.

Old habits die hard, Daniel thought, smiling, and then proceeded to go in. Their room was as he remembered it, with a large king-size bed in the middle with an elegant wooden bedframe. Something made Daniel's blood freeze. At first, he thought it was just background noise, but as he paid more attention to it, he realized the noise was familiar.

He left the room and looked down the hallway. A voice—a voice he hadn't heard in years. Daniel ran down the hallway and stood at the top of the stairs looking down, petrified. He saw Richard Spence playing with his favorite toy car.

The little boy looked up, with his typical innocent expression and big green eyes and dark hair.

"Hi, Captain Dan! Wanna play?"

Captain Dan…The name pierced Daniel's chest, generating a mixture of strong sadness and nostalgia. He stood there and smiled, holding back tears.

"Admiral Rick?" Daniel said with a broken voice as the first tear slid down his face.

He walked slowly down the stairs, and the smell of fresh bacon filled his nostrils. A sweet voice was humming in the kitchen. It was "Für Elise," by Beethoven, a song his mother always hummed while she cooked breakfast.

"Good morning, honey! You slept well?" A voice he had not heard in sixteen years, yet as familiar as his own, sent chills down his spine.

Daniel reached the bottom of the stairs and turned;

he saw Katherine Spence's pale face smiling at him. Her green eyes matched both Daniel's and Ricky's. Her long, brunette, undulating hair spread past her shoulders. Daniel stood there in between the living room and the kitchen, paralyzed by overwhelming emotions. The first, and strongest, was sadness, followed by happiness, mixing weirdly in his chest and stomach.

"Mom?" His voice sounded like a surprised but scared nine-year-old's.

"Yes, my dear?"

Daniel's face was covered in tears as he tried to say too much at once: "I love you."

"I love you too, Dani," Katherine responded in a sweet maternal voice.

Then he felt a soft pressure in his hip, and when he looked down, he saw Ricky hugging him and smiling at him. Daniel could not contain himself anymore, and now he was sobbing.

"Why are you crying, Captain Dan?" asked his little brother.

The sobs were stronger now, and it was hard to talk.

"I've wanted…this so bad…for so long, Ricky…I've…missed you." He looked at them and smiled. "I love you both. Please never forget that."

His mother walked toward him and hugged both of her sons. They all stayed like that for a long time.

CHAPTER 22

DANIEL SLOWLY OPENED his eyes. He sat up and tried to grasp everything that happened as he rubbed his face. That was when he felt the wetness and realized he had been crying in his sleep. Didn't matter. He had seen them, he said what he needed to say, but why was he brought back so abruptly right in the middle of everything?

"Welcome back, Mr. Spence," Dr. Cooper's voice came through the speaker.

"Why did you brought me back so quickly?" Daniel asked, looking at his serious face reflected in the mirror, trying to see Dr. Cooper in the Feeder Room.

"You did not notice it, did you? I guess that makes sense. You lowered your guard and were vulnerable. I can't really blame you. I've made the same mistake before."

"My guard? I was aware!"

"Did you notice the mud forming below your feet?"

The back of Daniel's neck felt hot. Mud? *I bet you can't reach the bottom.*

"You hugged them for a while, with you eyes closed, which blocked my view of what was happening. It was only when your mother spoke again that you opened them slightly, and that's when I saw it. I even have a recorded image—I'll show you."

Daniel did not need to see it to believe Dr. Cooper. How else would he have known of the mud at the bottom of the lake? The mud dripping from Ricky's dead hand.

The door opened behind him, and Daniel saw Dr. Cooper's reflection in the mirror, walking toward him. He placed his hand on Daniel's shoulder in a fatherly gesture. "How are you feeling, Mr. Spence?"

Daniel remained silent as he felt the last tear slide down his face. "I'm sorry," he said finally. "It's just a lot to digest."

"I know the feeling. But try and focus on the positive side—you saw them again. They are there, in the Reverie. They are there, just like my daughter. I could say this has been the most successful session I've had in years."

A heavy silence followed, until Daniel's serious tone broke it. "So what's the downside?"

Dr. Cooper took out a printed image and placed it in front of Daniel. It was black except for a groove on the right side. There, Daniel could see part of the kitchen of his wood cabin, and, as Dr. Cooper mentioned, mud that seemed to be flowing from nowhere.

"The mud you talked about…?"

"Look closer," the old man said patiently.

Daniel did. He saw the waves of mud that seemed to be approaching them. They weren't big; they would've probably covered their ankles at most. The kitchen seemed the same, with the wood cabinets and the large pantry.

Daniel felt dizzy when he saw it. That face, with the poached-egg white eyes and the large, creepy smile, was peeking from behind the pantry. You could barely see it, with only a fourth of the head visible, like a little kid peeking out as he hid behind a wall.

"It was…stalking us." His voice trembled.

"Yes. I believe it was going to attack soon."

"But why?"

"I wish I had an answer for you, Mr. Spence. That's why I think that if we can face it together, with both of our awareness capabilities maybe we can outpower it."

Daniel looked up at Dr. Cooper for the first time. "When do we start?" He was determined to get to the bottom of this. Anger filled his stomach: How did that monster dare touch his family? He would not allow it.

Dr. Cooper's eyes met Daniel's. "Good, then. We need to get the group together. Now that we have a clear goal, we can make the information available to them. They'll be monitoring the DSD while we go to the Reverie. We'll need all the help we can get." He walked toward the one-way mirror and stared into his reflected blue eyes. Then he shifted his gaze back to Daniel. "All right, then, I shall see you on Level Five, Room 5B, at seven thirty sharp."

Daniel started to take the electrodes off. "Sure…I can finish up here. You do not have to wait for me."

"Perfect. Great session, Mr. Spence."

Dr. Cooper tapped him on the shoulder and walked out. Daniel carried on, but the sound of the door shutting behind him made him stop. He held a red electrode up and inspected it, daring to think of something reckless, something insane, really. But between the solitude of that room and his crowded mind, strange, courageous ideas snuck in. What if he were to go…?

I bet you can't reach the bottom.

His own childish voice shut out the thoughts. He looked at his reflection for a couple of guilty seconds and continued to take the electrodes off.

"Good evening, everyone. I'd like to start by apologizing. I know I've been absent this past couple of weeks, but it was a necessary step. Thanks to that, tonight you'll learn the truth—all of it. This information is very, very delicate, which is why we are on Level Five, a space only I had access to until thirty minutes ago. I would not risk having this conversation anywhere else."

Dr. Cooper stood in front of all his researchers in a small conference room. Dr. Shoop sat to the left with his hands crossed and a serious expression on his face. Next to him, Dr. Cowen sat with straight, almost perfect posture as he listened carefully. Finally, Kelly Marshall sat toward the right, taking notes. Daniel sat facing the researchers, with Dr. Cooper to his right. He was not necessarily happy with his seat; it gave him a sense of authority he did not quite feel he deserved. But it was the old man's wish to have him there.

"From now on, I'll ask you all to please not record anything. I want to avoid any leakage." He looked at Kelly, who stopped writing and put the small notebook away. "I want to get everyone on the same page. Some of you might have more knowledge than others, so an overall review seems fit." Dr. Cooper went on to talk about the Reverie and the experiments he and Daniel had run to prove his theory. He left out some details, like the fact that he saw his dead daughter, or that Daniel saw his mom and brother. Instead, he mentioned that they found significant proof to demonstrate that this was a path worth pursuing.

"So, if we are in fact on the doorstep of another dimension, there could be a real risk. Starting with the creature we are all familiar with but we avoid talking about." He paused, expecting a question from his audience. "From now on, we'll call it the Dream Keeper." Kelly glanced at Daniel with a (*worried*) weird look. "We do not know the extent of its powers, but that is why Mr. Spence and I will go together. I've been training him as a lucid dreamer for some time, so my hypothesis is"—Dr. Cooper made hand gestures—"if the two of us can connect and interact while lucid in the Reverie, then we'll be able to have enough awareness to control the situation." He took a deep breath. "Let's hope it does not come down to that. Remember, our objective is to gather tangible evidence that demonstrates the existence of the Reverie."

He can't be serious. Our objective is to defeat and capture that monster.

He glanced at Daniel, as if almost reading his mind, so he decided to remain quiet. Then he carried on. "So here is the plan of action: Dr. Shoop, you'll be in the Receiver Room with us. I won't allow any nurses in."

"Dr. Cooper, may I ask why are you taking an intern with you on such a delicate journey?" Dr. Cowen, to whom Daniel had not paid much attention, looked a bit distressed.

Of course, it had to be Cowen.

Dr. Cooper took of his half-moon glasses and started cleaning them methodically. Then he spoke in a calm voice. "Are you questioning my judgment, Dr. Cowen?"

"N-no, sir, I was just wondering, if this is such a big

experiment, wouldn't it be better to take someone with a bit more experience?" His voice was slightly shaky, but he stood his ground.

"Experience?" He continued to focus on his glasses. "I've trained Mr. Spence myself. Are you implying that I did not prepare him well for this challenge?" Dr. Cooper looked up with a smile. Daniel was surprised by his tone. His voice was calm, but there was a bitter touch.

"No, sir," Dr. Cowen said in a low, defeated voice.

Dr. Cooper put his glasses back on and carried on. "Where was I? Ah yes, Dr. Shoop, you'll be in the Receiver Room with us. Dr. Cowen and Mrs. Marshall will be here in the Feeder. You'll monitor and make sure everything runs smoothly. You'll also be our extra pair of eyes. If you notice anything out of place, notify us. Use your judgment. If you see signs of imminent danger, wake us up. Ideally, we will be in and out before the Dream Keeper appears. But if it does, the three of you are responsible for bringing us back. Any questions?"

Kelly spoke first. "What should we do if we cut the gas and turn off the systems but you two don't wake up?"

"Dr. Shoop will be in the receiver side, so if necessary use physical force. He'll have cold water and other strong stimulants at hand in case we reach that point." He looked over at Dr. Shoop, who nodded. "If it comes down to that, I want you to bring Mr. Spence first. Make sure he is completely awake before bringing me back."

Daniel jumped. "Hold on, Dr. Cooper, I don't—"

He was stopped by a gesture from the old man. "I know what you are about to say, but those are my final instructions," he said in a calm but tired voice.

"Any other questions?" The room remained silent for a couple more seconds. "Perfect, I'm sure more will come up as we set everything up." Dr. Cooper took out his pocket watch and checked it. "It's almost nine p.m. Let's take a ten-minute break. Go gather any old notes you think you might need, then I want you all back here to get started on the setup. We go to the other side at ten p.m. Thanks, everybody."

Everyone stood up except Daniel, who saw the old man leaving the room first. He did not want a break; he was ready to go. So he decided to just linger until the break was over.

"Congratulations, Mr. Spence. This is very impressive," Dr. Shoop said as he extended his hand. Daniel quickly stood up and shook it back. "Oh, thanks."

A little smirk appeared on his face. "Since the moment I saw you I knew you were talented and destined to do great things."

Daniel smiled and could see over Dr. Shoop's shoulder how Kelly looked at him in a strange way from the other side of the room. She stood up next to Dr. Cowen, who was looking the other way, with his hands in his pockets.

"Well, thank you, Dr. Shoop. Hopefully something good will come out of all of this." As he talked, his focus was on Kelly, who avoided his gaze. As soon as she noticed, Daniel looked back.

What was that look for? Is she mad at me? Is it because I did not kept her up to date?

"Excuse me, I'm gonna get some fresh air."

He walked toward her, wanting to read her better. Dr. Cowen, who was reading something in his dream journal, saw him coming and walked the other way.

(*More of a favor than an insult, Cowen.*)

"Hey, how are you feeling?" Daniel asked.

"I'm good." The dry tone of her voice said otherwise. "Ready for your big moment?"

"I think so," Daniel said, placing his hands in his lab coat pockets. "Wanna smoke? We can get some fresh air."

"I'm sorry, Mr. Spence, Dr. Cowen asked me to help him with some calibrations. But you should go ahead. You have a long night ahead of you."

That was not the answer Daniel expected, but now he would look silly if he just stayed there. "Well, I'll be outside if you change your mind."

CHAPTER 23

THE SMOKE MOMENTARILY clouded Daniel's view of the beautiful, starry night. It reminded him of the weird psychedelic path on his way to his Core. The cold air brushed his face, bringing a clean smell from the trees. Up here, alone with his thoughts, Daniel had an entertaining discussion with himself. A mixture of anxiety and excitement brewed in his stomach as he went through all the possible outcomes in his head.

Best-case scenario: we manage to stop and defeat the Dream Keeper, and we collect enough evidence to prove the theory of the Reverie. Worst-case scenario? Who knows, really? A really bad nightmare? Or something worse, like what happened to Elizabeth?

Daniel took another puff and rubbed his face with his hands. He started to think, to recall his first day, the tour of the place, his first encounter...

Don't come!

Daniel looked around, confused.

"Hey, tough guy."

Daniel turned and saw Kelly walk through the revolving door of the lobby. "Are you ready?"

Don't...

Daniel heard it again and turned. It was a familiar voice that sounded distorted and felt like it came from far, far away.

"Ricky?" he whispered.

"What was that?" Kelly asked, reaching him.

"Nothing...Just my mind playing tricks. Is everything set downstairs?"

"Yes. Dr. Cooper sent me out to get you. Daniel are you sure—?"

"Yes, I am. We need to get to the bottom of this." He placed his hand on her shoulder. "Besides, I have you here, so I know that you have my back," Daniel said, smiling.

She looked down and said, "I'll do my best." She looked back up and lightly punched him on the chest. "But you better not get into too much trouble. Don't leave me alone with all these freaks." A half smile was drawn on her face.

Instinctively, Daniel hugged her. "I won't."

They hugged for some time. Daniel felt like he was in a very pleasant dream. Kelly never acted like this before.

She then pulled away slowly and looked at him for a couple of seconds. Daniel sensed something strange; Kelly seemed a bit...worried?

"Let's go. They are waiting."

"All right, let's do this."

"So, just make sure no gas is filtering out...Oh good, you are here. Feel free to take a seat," Dr. Cooper said, turning around. He stood next to one of the two medical chairs. Dr.

Shoop was to his right, leaning forward and taking notes. They both resumed their conversation shortly after.

Daniel smiled quickly and approached the other medical chair. He sat on it, felt its softness, and then looked toward the one-way mirror. He saw his reflection, but he hoped (*knew*) Kelly was looking back at him.

"All right. I believe we are ready," Dr. Cooper said calmly as he sat down on the other chair.

They faced each other awkwardly as Dr. Shoop started to connect the different pieces of medical equipment to monitor them.

"Remember your training, the abilities we've practiced. Try to keep in mind your dream journal as you fall asleep. That might trigger your awareness faster."

"Yes, got it."

"Now, one last thing. If we reach the point where they can't bring us back and we have to face it alone, this is what we are going to do: I'll use the glass walls you saw me use in my dream to delay its attack. While that's happening, you need to use the teleportation technique you used to go to your Core before to get away from there as quickly as possible. I'll deal with it myself, like I have multiple times in the past." The old man's face and tone were deadly serious.

"But maybe I could help. I know some techniques myself."

"Enough. That's my final decision. We are not discussing something that involves the physical or mental integrity of one of my researchers."

A tension almost as visible as fog could be felt in the room. Dr. Shoop momentarily stopped installing the gear, and Daniel felt heat in the back his neck and in his cheeks.

For a second, there was a heavy silence. Daniel wanted to argue more; he wanted to face the Dream Keeper, too, the source of his misery this past couple of months; the monster that stalked him in his most private moment of rejoicing with his family; the monster who marauded the same world his family was in. But Dr. Cooper's expression was intimidating.

"All right." His defeated tone spoke for him.

Dr. Cooper leaned back, removing some of the awkwardness from the room. Dr. Shoop carried on with the installation by placing the gas mask on Daniel and ensuring there were no leaks. Daniel felt the coldness of the glue used on the electrodes, the special glue they used to make them work around the hair. This was real; this was happening. Then Dr. Shoop leaned forward and glued one more red electrode to his forehead. Its cable was long, and on the other end there was another electrode, which Dr. Shoop later placed on Dr. Cooper's forehead. It was hard not to feel claustrophobic with all this equipment on him.

"Okay, we are all set." Dr. Shoop looked up.

"Are we ready?" Dr. Cowen asked through the speakers of the room.

Dr. Cooper gave a thumbs-up to the one-way mirror wall and looked at Daniel. The young intern looked back at his boss, and he could see the muscles in his face stretch into what seemed a smile below the gas mask. He smiled back, feeling better, and raised his thumb too. The strange smell of gas started flowing in, and his head fell back heavily. Slowly, Daniel slipped into a deep slumber.

The sand felt hot and the air was thick with an ocean smell. Daniel slowly opened his eyes and looked at the bright-blue sky. It seemed to be midday by how sunny it was, even though there was no sun to be seen. He sat up and looked around; sand and water surrounded him on all sides. It was as if he were on a small virgin beach in the middle of the Caribbean.

It's good to see you again
And finally meet you
The land of the free this is
So feel free to join in.

Daniel turned around and saw someone with a familiar face sitting close by. He could not remember where exactly he had seen this man, who was wearing rags, but he was sure it was recent.

"Hello. Ah…I'm Daniel. Have we met before?"

We have many times,
Although last time
You thought you'd hide
But it don't matter
As long as you ain't no thief.

Daniel saw that the man was drawing something with his finger in the sand. He was surprised at how realistic the drawing was: a boat with three kids that seemed to be traveling away from the water and into the stars above. He could almost see the color behind the shapes. Daniel stood up and shook the sand off his pants.

"I'm no thief. I'm sorry, where are we?"

The man looked up toward the horizon and smiled.

She comes when she wants
She protects what is hers
From the thieves from out there

The man looked away for a second, still smiling, and then continued drawing. The smile creeped Daniel out.

"Right."

He turned around to check what the man saw, but found nothing. Then he turned back and saw the man was gone, but the drawing remained in the sand. Daniel knelt next to it and inspected it. The level of detail was incredible. It almost seemed as if it were moving. But that was impossible. It was a drawing in the sand, unless…

He slowly moved his hand toward his pocket, unsure of what to expect, but following pure instinct. Then he felt it, a cubical shape.

The dream journal.

"Tha…ect," a loud voice spoke to him with a lot of static. Daniel jumped up and back, looking around.

"Dr. Cowen, please try to be more gentle. You even scared me with that tone of voice. Next time, wait until he is fully aware," the familiar calm voice came from behind him.

Daniel turned and saw Dr. Cooper walking toward him with a staff in his right hand and wearing his usual formal attire, with his lab coat and sunglasses.

"Oh, it's you, Dr. Cooper. What are you…?" Then the memories slowly started coming back.

"It's okay. Give it some time. You'll remember everything soon."

But "soon" was an understatement; all the memories hit Daniel like a train. He started to hyperventilate, realizing where he was and what he was doing.

"Relax, Mr. Spence. Remember your training. Here, have a seat," Dr. Cooper said as he sat down next to him on one of two very comfortable red couches. Daniel looked at his own couch, and sat down too, slowly recovering his breath. After a couple of minutes, he was more in control.

"I saw you having a little chat with Mr. Ollman."

"Who? Oh yes! That's where I know him from. He was one of the Natives from your dream, one with low awareness."

"That's right," he answered with a satisfied smile. "Interesting that of all the Natives I've known, he is the one who showed up first. Did he mention anything to you?"

"Just gibberish, honestly. Similar things to what he said to you, I believe."

"Good old Ollman. Always talking nonsense."

Daniel looked around and verified again that they were on an island in the middle of the ocean.

"Do you know where we are, Dr. Cooper?"

"We are in an old memory of mine…Yes, it's a memory of a beautiful virgin beach called Isla La Tortuga. It is located in Venezuela."

Daniel looked around again, this time paying attention to the details. He saw the crystal-clear water, with fish swimming around. He felt the warm, white sand with his bare feet.

"Why are we here?" Daniel asked, looking at the old man, who, strangely, looked and felt younger.

"I'm not sure. It's always random where you appear in your first dream, but this is definitely curious…Well, in any case, this was the first time we've manifested in the Reverie with another researcher. So this trip is already a success."

"I see. So, should we go collect samples? Find some sort of proof?"

Dr. Cooper turned to him, his lips slightly curved into a smirk. "Dr. Cowen, can you hear us?"

They stayed silent for a couple of seconds, awaiting a response. "They are probably having some trouble communicating. The objective is still the same one we discussed two nights ago. I did not say it explicitly to the researchers, because they do not really need to know."

"What do you mean?"

"Their objective is to keep us safe, and they are doing that following the instructions I gave them."

"But then why not just tell them the truth?"

"Because it does not make sense." Dr. Cooper stood up and looked out to the horizon. "Why would we come to the Reverie specifically looking for the main source of danger?"

"Because the monster is somehow connected to our families," Daniel said, pressing his fist hard.

"Exactly. But as you noticed, I did not mention anything about them. That's because they don't know anything about them." He turned to Daniel with a determined look on his face. "And I intend to keep it that way until we get to the bottom of this."

That was it. Everything finally clicked in Daniel's brain: Dr. Cooper did not want to show this was also personal. He did not want to show any sign of weakness. If that meant avoiding giving information that could possibly put his judgment in question, then so be it.

He is truly a fascinating man.

"I understand," Daniel said, standing up too. "So, what do we do now? Where can we find it?"

"D…opy…" the static voice spoke to both of them.

"There is too much static. Can you hear us?"

They both remained silent again, awaiting an answer that never came. Finally, Dr. Cooper turned around and stuck his walking stick in the sand.

"They will contact us soon, hopefully. Why don't we begin our journey and go find it, Dr. Cooper?" Daniel turned to look where Dr. Cooper was looking and saw that the beach now expanded back, with a clear path.

"I believe it will find us, Mr. Spence."

CHAPTER 24

AFTER A SHORT walk, the path became paved with stone, and it took them to a walled city that seemed to be a fort from the old West. On their way, Daniel created a walking stick using his awareness. Dr. Cooper congratulated him, and they went on to talk about the strategy they would use.

"Maybe we could start from one of our Cores and go from there," Daniel said, looking ahead.

"That could be an option, but if we do that, we should start with mine," Dr. Cooper said as he walked with his hands behind his back, as if giving a lecture. "You've only been to your Core once, so you are not very familiar with it. It'll be interesting to prove if someone different can manifest into another Core."

"What if…?"

"Dr. Cooper, can you hear me?" Dr. Cowen's voice seemed to come out of nowhere.

"Loud and clear," he said, smiling. "Took you guys some time to get synched up."

"Yeah, we had some issues with the frequencies, but we are all set now."

Daniel felt the urge to talk to Kelly but decided not to.

"Everything under control?" the old man asked.

"Yes, we can proceed," Dr. Cowen said.

"Daniel, hold my arm. We shall go to my Core and start there." He looked over at Daniel with a half smile. "Hope you are ready."

"Always," Daniel answered. The determination in his voice and eyes seemed to make Dr. Cooper proud. For whatever reason, Daniel felt a sense of accomplishment, even though he hadn't really achieved anything yet.

He grabbed his boss's arm and felt how old and fragile it really was. Then a force pulled him backwards in a sort of familiar way, and before he knew it he was flying with Dr. Cooper through the starry space he traveled through back in his own dream. They flew through the thick colored light, which changed colors from blueish green to violet to red. Daniel paid more attention to the details this time: through the colored light he could see millions of stars and shiny shapes.

As soon as a smile appeared on his face, the lights and shapes started to stretch out. Daniel looked up and could see they were approaching the Victorian house very fast from above. Instinctively, he covered his head with his free arm and prepared for the collision.

"You are fine, Mr. Spence. I know it takes some time to get used to it," Dr. Cooper said in his usual calm voice.

Daniel uncovered himself, looked around, and realized he was in the lobby. "Dr. Cowen, how are we looking?"

"Nothing to worry about, sir."

"Good. I believe we've made it, Mr. Spence. You are officially manifesting in my Core."

Daniel was impressed by the beautiful marble with golden ornaments and statues. The gold handrails from the center stairs were like open arms welcoming the guest, with dawn sunlight that filtered through the windows giving the space a reddish hue. Daniel had seen it before, of course, through a screen, but knowing he was now standing here was…Well, it was like a reverie.

"Henry, what have you done?" a familiar voice came from the upper level.

A couple of seconds later, a tall black man wearing a long black leather jacket appeared and started to go down the stairs.

"Philemon, I do not have time for you right now," Dr. Cooper said patiently, and took a step forward.

Daniel remembered him and saw the indentation in his forehead.

"You will breach the laws of this nature. She is coming for you. She is coming for you both."

"Dr. Cooper, what is—?"

"Silence, intruder!" Philemon yelled at Daniel, and his third yellow eye opened. "You don't understand this land or its rules. You are just a child." His eye looked at Dr. Cooper, who was waving both hands in a circular motion. "Stop this, Henry. I know you. You are better…" He stopped halfway and turned around. "She is here."

Daniel saw how the light slowly dimmed, and in a matter of seconds night came. Just a bit of moonlight filtered through the windows of the lobby. Philemon's eye was now the strongest source of light in the space.

"Dr. Co— , losing…" Dr. Cowen's voice was now pure static.

"Daniel, stay close to me," Dr. Cooper said.

"You need to leave now!" Philemon said as he turned. The light emanating from his eye shone to the top floor. There his face was, with its uncanny smile, twitching a little.

Daniel felt a cold breeze around him and realized the house was now melting. He stood next to Dr. Cooper, fear slowly crawling up his back. Suddenly, the light from the eye shut off, and a piercing sound bounced off the melting walls, followed by the sound of a heavy fall on the stairs.

A darkness covered everything, and for a moment the only thing he could hear was Dr. Cooper breathing next to him.

"I've never seen this much control before," Dr. Cooper said.

Fluorescent lights turned on. They provided white light that gave a clear view of what seemed to be a long hallway of a very old house. Daniel took a step forward and realized there was water all the way to his ankles. "Do you know where we are?" he asked with a trembling voice.

"I'm not sure. But wherever it is, is where the Dream Keeper wants us to be."

"Why haven't we woken up? Isn't Dr. Shoop supposed to be there to use physical means to bring us back?" Daniel asked, his voice bordering hysterical.

The sound of splashing steps interrupted them. They were fast, one after the other, coming from afar.

"I'm sorry!" came from behind.

Daniel turned and saw another familiar face: Dr. Cooper's daughter.

"Olivia," the old man said, and he stepped forward, but as she reached him, she dodged his hug and ran toward

Daniel. She embraced him with a tender force and started crying. Daniel looked down, confused.

"Hey, little one, what's wrong?" he asked, placing a hand on her back.

She looked up with tears running down her pink cheeks. "I tried to warn you not to come, but it was too hard. Now…" She wept between words, which made it hard to understand her. "Now is too late…"

Daniel felt her let go, and her eyes slowly closed. He saw her falling backwards and quickly kneeled to grab her. He looked up at Dr. Cooper, disconcerted. The old man quickly knelt, too, and grabbed his daughter with careful tenderness.

"Captain Dan…" The trembling voice made Daniel's skin crawl. He looked back up and saw something that froze every inch of his body. The Dream Keeper stood just a few feet ahead; in front was his little brother.

"Ricky!" He stood up. "Let him go! This is between you and me."

The Dream Keeper's eerie smile did not change. Its head tilted slightly to the left; its white eyes met Daniel's. The fluorescent lights started to flicker, and suddenly Daniel saw pictures of what was happening. One long, sharp finger slid down the faces of the crying kids.

I bet you can't reach the bottom.

"*No!*" Daniel yelled, and ran toward his little brother.

But the space was playing tricks on him. What seemed to be just a few feet kept stretching back. He saw how the finger slowly moved from the cheek into the left side of his neck. Daniel ran as hard as he could, but he did not advance one inch. Then the Dream Keeper slowly slit Ricky's throat.

Pure horror—that thick, black substance that comes from the most primitive part of our human nature—boiled in Daniel's chest. It was in every cell of his body, paralyzing him. Thick blood spurted out of Ricky's half-cut neck as the creature held its chin up, and his body slowly leaned forward. The grotesque scene and the smile of the Dream Keeper sparked in Daniel's stomach. Suddenly, all the thick, black substance became powder that fed the fire of hate. Every inch of his body screamed with an irrational anger that pushed Daniel forward in a frenzy.

"*I'm going to kill you!*" Daniel yelled with all the anger and hate he had in him.

The hallway stopped stretching, and in a couple of seconds he reached the Dream Keeper, who threw Ricky's body to the side. Daniel closed his hand, and with an iron fist he punched the creature's face.

It felt like punching a wall. The Dream Keeper did not move, nor did its expression change. Daniel felt the coldness of its dry skin on his fist, and, with a disbelieving expression, listened as the creature laughed. The sound was a familiar one, almost like a metallic croaking.

Daniel saw everything in a sort of slow motion, thanks to the flickering lights. The Dream Keeper opened its mouth, a large black hole with dozens of sharp teeth, and bit Daniel's arm off. Before he could scream, a sharp, unbearable pain cut his voice. Daniel looked down, as blood slid out of his mouth, at how the Dream Keeper's arm had pierced his chest.

CHAPTER 25

His GASPS FOR air echoed off the walls of the long hallway. Daniel saw Ricky's lifeless body in the water. He was losing blood rapidly as he struggled to breathe and wheezed. Tears slid down his cheeks as he started to see black-and-silver spots in his vision.

"All right, that's enough," Dr. Cooper's voice came from behind.

Daniel saw a glass wall had formed between him and the Dream Keeper. It cut the creature's arm, and Daniel fell backwards. He landed on the arm of Dr. Cooper, who set him down on the floor with his back resting against the wall.

"You did great, Mr. Spence. Let me take this off."

The old man kneeled next to Daniel and, with a steady hand, pulled the arm out of his chest. Daniel screamed in excruciating pain.

"I know. I'll help you, Mr. Spence. I'll…"

But the old man did not finish the sentence. His gaze rested on Daniel's chest wound. A dim silver light shone back on his face as the moribund Daniel gasped for air and started shaking. Behind them, the Dream Keeper suddenly became very violent, trying to break the glass box that trapped it with its head and remaining arm.

"Help! Please!" Daniel begged.

But Dr. Cooper's expression was different. He had a look of pure satisfaction as he regarded the silver light.

"Such is the irony of this dimension. The one thing I was looking for was not on the Dream Keeper but unintentionally given to me by it. For years I've been researching, fighting, and pushing to find it: a soul." His voice was almost maniacal now, and he had a wide grin as he gazed down at the silver light coming from Daniel's chest.

Over the sound of the Dream Keeper hitting the glass frenetically, a barely audible whisper came out of Daniel's mouth. "What?...Why?"

Dr. Cooper looked over at his daughter's lifeless body, then down at Daniel, no trace of emotion on his face. The old man leaned forward and spoke into Daniel's ear.

"I'm sorry it had to be this way, Mr. Spence, but you fit the profile: young, bright man tormented by his past stole drugs from the lab to get high. But in his last round he went too far and overdosed...You grew on me quite a bit and proved to be a fine apprentice. Your determination set you apart from every other researcher I've ever worked with but in the end also sealed your fate. I must say it's been an honor, Mr. Spence." He leaned back up, rolled up his shirtsleeves, and with his hand covered the silver light in Daniel's chest. He pulled, sending a last wave of pain to Daniel's brain, and after a few struggles everything went black.

Dr. Cooper stood and held up a round silver sphere. The Dream Keeper was now in a frenzy, hitting the cracking glass walls that surrounded it with his hand and head. The old man walked toward the creature, who momentarily stopped and looked at the soul, still with its characteristic grin.

"Stop it. You won't break loose for another hour. We've been through this already. Although last time I let you catch me. So, I guess it's fair I had my revenge."

The Dream Keeper looked at him and continued frantically punching the wall. Dr. Cooper simply walked away.

"Dr. Cowen, can you hear me?"

"Loud and clear, sir."

"Good. Let's proceed to phase two. Is my daughter ready?"

"Yes, sir. Dr. Shoop set her up. We just need to transport you."

"Make sure you don't wake me up." He raised his hand to give the soul another look. "Isn't it beautiful, Viktor?" Dr. Cooper said in a tired but triumphant tone as he created a comfy chair and sat on it. He looked at the creature's white eyes and smiled, ignoring the fact that the creature's missing arm was slowly crawling through the water behind them. It was slowly moving toward Daniel's body.

"Indeed it is, sir. Everything has gone according to plan."

"It has, but let's not get ahead of ourselves."

"Oh yes, sorry, Dr. Cooper. Dr. Shoop just came back to the Receiver Room."

Dr. Cooper stood up and put his hands behind his back, with the silver sphere shining between his fingers. "Terrific. Today is…" But his statement was cut short. His words were replaced by a shriek. Blood flowed out of his mouth. He took a step forward and then kneeled as the blood dripped down his shirt. With his free hand, he tried to find the source of the immense pain coming from his stomach.

"*Dr. Cooper!*" Dr. Cowen screamed, followed by static.

The old man gasped for air, but he slowly realized he was not looking into the Dream Keeper's white eyes in the hallway anymore. He was awake back in the Receiver Room, looking down; looking at how Daniel Spence's arm had pierced him through his stomach. Dr. Cooper looked to his left and saw the terrified look in Dr. Shoop's eyes. But the former was not looking at him but at Daniel, and as he looked over, he saw the last thing he would see in his life: plain white eyes and a grin so big it was almost unnatural on Daniel's face.

"*You did not trap all of me, old man,*" Daniel said in a mixture of voices. The voice was partially his, but there was also another voice, one that wasn't human. "And this time it's not just a dream where you'll wake up."

He stood up and, with a quick movement of his hand, jerked out Dr. Cooper's guts, which splattered all over the floor. Daniel grabbed the old man by his neck, raised him up, disconnecting most of the electrodes from his head, then threw him across the room. His body collided with the glass wall and cracked it. Dr. Cooper dropped to the floor and never moved again.

Dr. Shoop, who saw the whole thing, was petrified on the floor. He had fallen backwards when Daniel stood up. He crawled for the door, then tried to stand and run. The Dream Keeper moved with unnatural agility and grabbed Dr. Shoop's blond hair.

"I'm sorry! I was just following orders!" he begged as he struggled. The Dream Keeper held his hair tight and dragged him back, walking awkwardly. It lifted him up in front of the one-way mirror. Dr. Shoop struggled to free himself, but it was no good. He was crying and yelling for help as he saw the eerie smile reflected in the mirror. Then, slowly, the Dream Keeper reached his throat and ripped it out, splattering blood all over the mirror.

For a moment, everything went dark, and then red lights turned on as the alarm went off. But Daniel's blank eyes looked at the bloody one-way mirror wall. The job was not done yet. With a quick motion, he turned, grabbed one of the medical chairs, and with inhuman force, lifted it and threw it at the bulletproof glass wall. It shattered, and he jumped through it, landing on the DSD keyboard. He saw only Dr. Cowen, who was crawling backwards into the corner of the room. A trickle of blood slid down his forehead. The Dream Keeper could see thick, black horror on his face, and its smile got wider. Slowly and awkwardly, it walked toward him, enjoying every second of the end of this bastard.

The door behind him burst open, and more red light spilled into the room.

"*Freeze!*"

"*Shoot him!*" Dr. Cowen yelled desperately.

But the Dream Keeper did not care…No, it had a job to finish. It raised Daniel's leg and, with a quick jerk, stomped Dr. Cowen's skull against the corner, smashing it into pieces.

A shot was fired and hit Daniel's shoulder. It turned around and saw a group of five security men pointing guns at him.

"No! Don't hurt him please! Don't…!" Kelly yelled in a scared, high-pitched voice. She stood behind the men in the hallway with her hands behind her back.

The Dream Keeper tilted its head, always with that eerie smile on its face, and then attacked.

EPILOGUE

THE THICK MANILA folder made a loud sound as it landed in the middle of the desk between the two women. On one side of the desk, Kelly Marshall, former intern at The Cooper Institute. On the other, a tall blond women in a nice suit.

"Evening. My name is Claudia Rodriguez. I'm the director of special research. Let's see," she said as she opened the manila folder and took out a set of papers. "On Monday, June the twelfth, 1995, Dr. Cooper conducted a highly dangerous experiment that included his whole research crew. There are no files or evidence of the purpose of this experiment. No audio, no film, nothing. The old man did a great job at covering his tracks." She closed the folder and looked at Kelly, who looked down at the desk. "The only evidence we have is sitting right in front of me. Can we work together to untangle this mess?"

The last sentence brought Kelly back. "Mess? That's a bit of an understatement, don't you think?" she asked in a loud voice, looking up.

"I understand that you are upset. You went through a

really thick one and barely came out of it alive. Not counting all the grief you are probably feeling."

Kelly gave her a penetrating look. "Grief? You really think I'm grieving for those monsters? They were the ones who caused all of this, starting with the man who used to sit in that chair not forty-eight hours ago!" She then realized she was yelling and felt ashamed. Since when did she show her emotions like that?

"I'd suggest some caution—after all, I'm your new boss, at least for the time being. I can understand your emotions are…turbulent. But I have a job to do. This informal interview was scheduled to determine if you are still fit to work at The Cooper Institute—at least for the time being." Her voice was calm and rational yet direct.

"Me? So you guys are not shutting this place down?" Kelly asked suspiciously.

She turned the chair to the left and leaned back a bit. "Well, that's where things get a bit…complicated. I fought to keep this place alive for the next two months. My supervisors did put up some resistance, but after a good fight, they gave me what I asked for."

"But why?"

"The official version is that there was a lot of data and cleanup that needed to be done before we could shut this off." The woman leaned forward and spoke in a soft, low voice. "But to tell you the truth, I still see a lot of potential here. After seeing the scene and having the surviving officer describe what happened, I knew I was onto something."

"This is insane. You are trying to keep up with one of the brightest, most twisted minds of our time. You really think you can continue Dr. Cooper's research?"

"Not on my own," she said, placing both hands on the table. "You worked with the guy for almost ten months. Not only that, but based on your file, you helped with a lot of his organization. And most importantly, you are the only survivor of the last failed experiment. So, you probably know a good chunk of that, don't you?"

"I'm not interested."

Claudia leaned back, keeping her eyes on Kelly's. "Here I was thinking I could be talking to the old man's replacement. But I get it: you are a pragmatic woman, and I respect that." She remained silent for a couple of seconds and exchanged looks with Kelly. Then after some sort of internal debate, she carried on. "Before you make a final decision, let me show you one thing. Please follow me." She stood and led Kelly out of the office.

The two women stood in front of a room without a number on Level 3. There were two guards, one on each side of the door. Before Claudia swiped the door open, she looked back at Kelly.

"I must warn you. What you are about to see will shock you."

Kelly nodded, and Claudia swiped in. They were inside a feeder room. There wasn't anything different from the other rooms, except for two people with unfamiliar faces sitting by the DSD keyboard. A ginger chubby man with a trimmed beard and an Asian man with a small nose looked at her with some disbelief. She looked at them and then look toward the receiver side. What she saw made her sick: Daniel Spence lay strapped to a medical bed, his head, right shoulder, chest, and left arm wrapped in gauze. He was connected to a mechanical ventilator machine and a heart monitor.

"No," Kelly said in a thin whisper.

"Yes, Mr. Spence was shot five times. In the right shoulder, in the left arm, and three times in the chest. It should have been fatal, but instead he entered a coma. We still can't explain how or what happened to him." They both looked at the young man for some time.

"So, what? You want to bring me on board to experiment with my coworker?"

"Oh no, Mrs. Marshall, I don't want you on board. I want you in charge."

Kelly's eyes widened, and she turned toward Claudia.

The tall, beautiful woman approached Kelly. "Yes, I can't think of anyone more qualified to help us here than Dr. Cooper's direct and only surviving researcher. The answers are all in there," she said, pointing at Daniel. "We just need someone to lead us in the right direction."

Kelly looked back toward Daniel and remained quiet for some time. The room seemed to go completely silent, and for a moment she felt alone.

"So, what do you say? Are you gonna go back to grad school, or are you gonna stay with us and make history?"

Kelly approached the DSD keyboard and slid her fingers over the keys. She took a deep breath and looked up. "Let's begin."

AFTERWORD

IN MY FIRST draft of *The Dream Keeper*, I gave Daniel Spence something that I myself needed in my time of greatest struggle: a best friend. His name was Marcus, and he met Daniel when they were little kids, before the laws of society and the hormones kicked in during the teenage years. Their friendship was one of the purest things I've written, because it was based on a true friendship and a true best friend: Marcos Hirschfeld.

Like Daniel and Marcus, we met when we were really young, probably around six years old. At the time, my life was marred by the divorce of my parents, and I had been through tough times no kid should go through. I remember sitting next to this goofy-looking kid on the bus. I was a quiet, very shy, and insecure kid, but for some unexpected reason he started to talk to me. We then went on to talk about all sorts of things that I can't remember, except for one. I remember we even talked about X-Men and agreed on it being the best cartoon, when in reality I had no idea what the X-Men were or what we were talking about, but I played along because I was happy to talk to someone, I was happy to have someone. Strange as it is, I remember that moment clearly, and that marked the beginning of our friendship. Marcos became the one friend I could rely on unconditionally.

Like Daniel and Marcus's friendship, ours became stronger over the years, and just like Marcus lived Daniel's traumas as if they were his own, and supported his friend through thick and thin, Marcos lived my traumas and listened to me when no one else would, and was there with me through the most tumultuous time of my life. He was the shoulder I could cry on no matter the time or place or our age, and his family always welcomed me with open arms and pure love.

Marcos was one of the most talented people I knew when it came to art and expression. He could translate an abstract thought into a beautiful sketch with meaning and soul. When I started writing, I called him and told him about it. Not only was he excited but we also talked about future projects, trilogies I wanted to write, and how he would do the concept art for them. We had all these plans, but life had a different idea. Marcos passed away in February 2018.

It happened around a year after I started writing. By then he had given me a lot of feedback on the design of the cover, allowing me to achieve the astonishing result you now have in your hands. He also helped me whenever I needed an idea or a different perspective for a scene. It didn't matter what it was or when I asked him; he was always there for me.

February 9 was the hardest day of my life, a day when my whole world was shaken to its core, and even my will to write shut down. But I knew that I had to finish this book, not only for me, but for him too. He was and still is part of this journey, and now I have the chance to immortalize his name.

I must be honest here. I don't feel like I'm doing justice to all the good Marcos brought to this world. I don't think a thousand pages would be enough to describe what he did, not only because of how much he did, but the meaning of it as well. I want this to be known: Marcos Hirschfeld was an amazing, caring, loving, free-spirited person. He was always smiling, always relaxing, always listening, always there for others. To sum it up, he was always living and loving others.

My first friend, my brother by choice, I miss you every day. But I can tell you that your flame is bright and strong in all of us. The day you passed was the day we all took the unspoken vow to keep living to the fullest and remembering you as an example of pure joy and love.

Now, to you, dear reader, who has made it this far, I can only say thank you for allowing me to share such a personal thing with you. And now I'm going to ask for one last thing: vow to live life to the fullest, love with passion, and be there for your loved ones. Even though you might not have known Marcos, the message he left behind is universal.

Thank you.

We did it, brother.